PICK YOUR POISON

"Do you have families?"

Clogburn cocked his head. "What if we do?"

"You need to ask yourselves if they can get along without you."

"You dirty cur," the third man said. "Trying to scare us into not doing our jobs."

"You're not real lawmen," Fargo said.

"We were deputized," Clogburn said. "We took an oath and swore to uphold the law." He held out a hand. "Now let's have that smoke wagon, or else."

Fargo knew a lost cause when he heard one. These men weren't his enemies, but he'd be damned if he'd let them take him in and more damned if he'd turn his hardware over to them. "It will have to be the 'or else.'"

"You picked it," Clogburn said. He looked at the other two and nodded.

They drew, or at least they started to.

Not one had cleared his holster when the Colt was in Fargo's hand. He fanned a shot into Clogburn's shoulder and another into the deputy on the right and a third into the last.

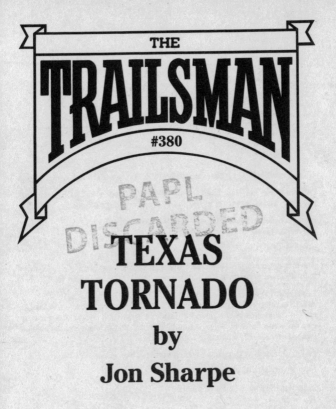

THE TRAILSMAN

#380

TEXAS TORNADO

by

Jon Sharpe

A SIGNET BOOK

SIGNET
Published by the Penguin Group
Penguin Group (USA) Inc., 375 Hudson Street,
New York, New York 10014, USA

USA | Canada | UK | Ireland | Australia | New Zealand | India | South Africa | China

Penguin Books Ltd, Registered Offices: 80 Strand, London WC2R 0RL, England
For more information about the Penguin Group visit penguin.com.

First published by Signet, an imprint of New American Library,
a division of Penguin Group (USA) Inc.

First Printing, June 2013

The first chapter of this book previously appeared in *Hangtown Hellcat*, the three
hundred seventy-ninth volume in this series.

ISBN 978-0-451-41757-2

Printed in the United States of America
10 9 8 7 6 5 4 3 2 1

ALWAYS LEARNING   PEARSON

The Trailsman

Beginnings . . . they bend the tree and they mark the man. Skye Fargo was born when he was eighteen. Terror was his midwife, vengeance his first cry. Killing spawned Skye Fargo, ruthless, cold-blooded murder. Out of the acrid smoke of gunpowder still hanging in the air, he rose, cried out a promise never forgotten.

The Trailsman they began to call him all across the West: searcher, scout, hunter, the man who could see where others only looked, his skills for hire but not his soul, the man who lived each day to the fullest, yet trailed each tomorrow. Skye Fargo, the Trailsman, the seeker who could take the wildness of a land and the wanting of a woman and make them his own.

Texas, 1861—a town wants to clap Fargo in leg irons, but they'll do it over his dead body.

1

The baying of hounds keened in the hot, muggy air of a Texas afternoon.

Skye Fargo drew rein to listen. A big man, broad at the shoulder, slender at the hips, he wore buckskins and a white hat brown with dust. A red bandanna around his neck lent a splash of color. In a holster nestled a Colt that had seen a lot of use, and snug in a boot, hidden from prying eyes, was an Arkansas toothpick. The stock of a Henry rifle jutted from his saddle scabbard.

The baying grew louder.

He figured a hunter was after game. Maybe a deer, maybe an antelope, although dogs had little hope of catching one.

Fargo was in a part of Texas he had never been to before, a sea of grassy plain broken here and there by rolling hills. Comanches roamed there, and killed any whites they came across. That hadn't stopped the white man, though, from establishing settlements and even a few towns.

Judging by the tracks and wagon ruts Fargo had come across, he knew there was one up ahead. He reckoned to stop and treat himself to a few drinks before pushing on.

From the crest of a low hill, he could see for half a mile or more out across the plain. His lake blue eyes narrowed when he caught sight of a lone figure running in his direction. The animal the hounds were after, he reckoned.

Then he realized the figure was on two legs, not four.

Fargo stayed put. Long ago he'd learned not to stick his nose into affairs that didn't concern him.

The figure came on fast but not fast enough. The hounds appeared, far back. They were gaining. Now and then they bayed.

"None of my concern," Fargo said to the Ovaro.

The stallion had its ears pricked and was staring intently at the unfair race.

Then Fargo glimpsed flowing brown hair, and it hit him that the figure was a woman in a shirt and britches. Just like that, everything changed. A tap of his spurs brought the stallion to a trot. He descended the hill and rode to intercept her.

The woman was losing steam. She weaved and staggered and slowed and stopped. That she had run for so long in that awful heat was remarkable. Now it was taking its toll.

Head down, she was breathing in great gasps, a hand pressed to her side. She was unaware of Fargo until he was almost on top of her.

Snapping erect, her hazel eyes filling with fear, she cried out, "No! I won't let you!"

Fargo liked what he saw. She had an oval face, lovely as could be, and an equally striking figure, which her baggy shirt and loose pants couldn't conceal. He smiled and said, "I don't aim to hurt you, ma'am. Are you in some sort of trouble?"

"What?" she said, as if she hadn't heard right.

"Those dogs," Fargo said, with a nod at the approaching hounds.

"What?" she said again.

Farther back, Fargo noticed, were several men on horseback.

"Oh God," she said, and hope replaced her fear. "You're not from there, are you?"

"From where?"

"Fairplay," the woman said.

2

"Never heard of it."

The woman glanced over her shoulder, and blanched. Suddenly she came to the Ovaro and gripped his leg with surprising strength. "Please," she said. "Get me out of here."

"What's this all about?" Fargo wanted to know. "Why are those men after you?"

"I don't have time to explain." She held fast with both hands. "I'm begging you. Help me up and ride like the wind."

Fargo would have been the first to admit he had a weakness for a pretty face. He was about to lower his arm and swing her up when his gaze fell on the men on horseback. The gleam of metal on a vest gave him pause. "Are those lawmen?"

"They're animals," the woman said. "The whole town." Tears filled her eyes, and desperation her voice. "For God's sake, take me out of here before it's too late."

It already was.

The four hounds arrived in a flurry of legs and tails. The foremost, a big brute with floppy ears and a mouth brimming with teeth, made straight for the woman. Its intention was clear, and it coiled to spring.

Fargo drew and fanned a shot from the hip. He didn't shoot the dog, not when the law was involved. He fired into the ground in front of it, and the hound veered and yipped and came to a stop. So did the rest of the pack.

Fargo held the Colt ready to shoot again if the dogs came at her, but they stood there growling and looking from him to her, uncertain what to do.

The three riders were at a gallop.

Turning with her back to the Ovaro, the woman let out a sob and clutched at her throat. "Oh God," she said. "Oh God, oh God, oh God."

Fargo had been right; all three riders wore tin stars.

The man in the lead had a belly that bulged over a wide belt and a moon face that glistened with sweat. A short-brimmed hat looked too small for his big head. His pudgy right hand rested on a hip above one of a matched pair of Starr revolvers. He brought his bay to a stop and scowled. Looking at the hounds, he said, "I thought you shot one, mister."

Fargo still held his Colt low and level. "All I did was stop them from chewing on the lady."

The dogs raised their heads to the man with the belly as if awaiting his command to attack.

"It's a good thing you didn't hurt them," the tin star said. "It'd have gone hard for you, interfering with a posse." His dark eyes fixed on the Colt. They were twin points of flint, those eyes, and didn't match his pudgy body.

Since none of the three had resorted to a gun, Fargo twirled his into his holster.

"Slick," the lawman said. He glared at the woman. "I'll get to you in a minute, Carmody."

The woman mewled like a frightened kitten.

"Now, then," the pudgy man with the hard eyes said. "I'm Marshal Luther Mako. These are my deputies, Clyde and Gergan."

Fargo took an immediately dislike to both. Clyde was a rat in clothes. Gergan was skinny enough to be a rake handle. Both looked as if they wanted to take a bite out of him.

"And you might be?" Marshal Mako asked when Fargo didn't respond.

Fargo gave them his handle. He half reckoned they might have heard of him, given the times he'd been written up in the newspapers. But they didn't act is if they had. "I scout for a living," he mentioned. Mostly.

"Do you know Carmody Wells here?" Marshal Mako asked with a bob of his fleshy chin at the terrified woman.

"I never set eyes on her before today."

"She's an escaped prisoner. She broke out of jail and—"

"Not jail!" Carmody cried. She turned to Fargo, her face twisted in appeal. "Don't listen to him. He lies with every breath. You have to help me or I'm done for."

4

Marshal Mako leaned on his saddle horn and sighed. "Broke custody, then. Does that sound better?" He looked at Fargo and sadly shook his head. "She was sentenced to six months at hard labor."

"A woman?" Fargo said.

"It's not as bad as it sounds," Marshal Mako said. "She helps with the cook wagon that goes out and feeds the work crews."

"Work crews!" Carmody said. "Men in chains is more like it."

"Lawbreakers," Mako said. "Duly put on trial and found guilty." He motioned at the deputies. "Enough of this. Tie her and let's head back."

Clyde and Gergan began to climb down.

Carmody Wells reached up and seized Fargo's hand.

"*Please*," she begged. "Don't let them take me. They'll whip me for sure."

Marshal Mako let out another sigh. "I've never whipped anybody, lady, and you know it." To Fargo he said, "She was arrested for stealing and resisting arrest. She tried to stab Gergan there. And there were witnesses."

"I didn't steal anything," Carmody said. "Honest."

The deputies walked up on either side of her.

"Come along peaceable, ma'am," Gergan said.

"We don't want to hurt you," Clyde assured her.

Carmody recoiled like a bobcat at bay. She clawed at Clyde's face and he ducked. In a bound she was past him, but he flung out a leg and she tripped and fell. Before she could rise, they had her by the arms.

"Gently, boys," Marshal Mako said. "Don't hurt her if you can help it."

Fargo felt sorry for her, but he wasn't about to buck a tin star without good cause, and from the sound of things, the marshal was only doing his job.

"Come along quietly, Carmody," Mako said. "It'll be easier on you."

Carmody did no such thing. She tugged and pulled and kicked. It was all Gergan and Clyde could do to hold on to her. She landed on Clyde's shin a good kick, which made him yelp, and tried to plant her other foot between Gergan's legs.

"Calm down!" Marshal Mako commanded.

Carmody fought harder. She drove a knee into Gergan's gut, doubling him over, and was on the verge of wrenching loose from Clyde when Marshal Mako gigged his mount and with a flick of his arm rapped her over the crown of her head with a pistol barrel.

Fargo was impressed. He'd barely seen the lawman's hand move. "Slick," he said.

Mako stared at the unconscious form on the ground. "I hated to do that. I truly did." He hefted his revolver, then shoved it into its holster. "I don't like hitting women, but she brought it on herself."

"A man does what he has to," Fargo said.

"I'm glad you see it that way." Mako ordered his deputies to bind her, then had them place her belly down over Gergan's saddle. Gergan was told to ride double with Clyde back to town.

"How about you, mister?" the lawman asked Fargo. "Care to pay Fairplay a visit?"

"Is it a dry town?"

Mako chuckled. "We have two saloons with all the liquor you could want."

"That's a lot," Fargo said.

"Then come ahead," Marshal Mako said cheerfully. "You'll find we're about the friendliest town this side of anywhere."

The woman called Carmody Wells groaned.

2

The plain ahead became lush with grass and cattle. Hundreds of head, grazing, or resting and chewing their cuds. Dozens of calves frolicked, unaware their nimble agility would soon give way to the ponderous bulk of age.

Marshal Mako brought them to a winding track of a road that cut through the high grass toward buildings silhouetted against the blue sky.

"Fairplay," the lawman said. He gazed out over the peaceful scene and said as if it were his, "A slice of paradise on earth."

To Fargo it was obvious. "You like it here."

"I've never liked anywhere more," Mako admitted. "It fits me like a glove."

Presently they came on a wagon parked at the side of the road. A burly man with a shotgun across his lap sat on the seat, his cheek bulging with a thick wad of tobacco. He spat over the side, wiped his mouth with a sleeve, and said, "Howdy, Marshal."

"Howdy yourself, Travers," Mako said. "Are they behaving today?"

"They'd better."

The "they" referred to were seven men in striped outfits, who were engaged in digging a ditch. With every movement, chains clamped to their ankles clattered.

Two other men stood guard, watching with the restless eyes of a pair of cats overseeing mice.

"So Carmody Wells was right," Fargo remarked.

"Never said she wasn't," Marshal Mako said, and nodded at the prisoners. "All duly tried and convicted and serving their time."

"Fairplay is a prison town?" Fargo knew that work gangs like this were a common practice at prisons.

"What makes you say that?" Mako said, then shook his head. "Oh no. They're housed at the barracks at the jail."

Fargo had never heard of a jail with a barracks before. He brought that up.

Marshal Mako shrugged. "It's just what we call it. We don't have a prison of our own, and the closest is hundreds of miles away and it wouldn't do to send them there."

The men in chains, Fargo noticed, cast hate-filled glances at the lawman and the deputies—but were careful to do so when none of the tin stars or the guards was looking.

"We might need our own prison soon, though," Deputy Clyde said with a chuckle, "the way things are going."

"How do you mean?" Fargo asked.

Luther Mako answered before the deputy could. "We've had a spate of crime lately."

Fargo rose in the stirrups and studied the silhouettes. He guessed there were at least thirty buildings that he could see with more beyond. "How big is this town of yours?"

Marshal Mako shrugged again. "Don't know as anyone has bothered to count in a while. Last I heard, about one hundred souls, more or less."

Fargo did the arithmetic in his head. Seven men in chains plus Carmondy made for eight. It seemed a high number for a town that size.

They rode on. Soon a large ranch house reared on the right. Set a hundred yards or so back from the road, it was shaded by tall trees and flanked by a stable and outhouses with recent coats of paint. In a field to one side, five men in striped clothes were using hoes to dig holes and plant seeds.

"*More* prisoners?" Fargo said.

"We've got about twenty, altogether," Marshal Mako said matter-of-factly. "The rest are working on municipal projects."

Mako didn't strike Fargo as the sort of hombre who went around throwing out words like "municipal." It started him pondering.

Just then a carriage appeared, coming toward them from town, pulled by a fine team in resplendent harness. The driver wore a bright green outfit with gold braid at the shoulders, and a peaked hat.

"What the hell?" Fargo said.

The lawmen and the deputies reined to one side and came to a stop.

"Make way," Mako said.

Fargo obliged him and reined over. "Who's in there, the governor?" he joked.

"Someone a heap more important around these parts," Marshal Mako said. "Horatio Stoddard."

"Never heard of him," Fargo admitted.

"He's the town's founding father," the lawman said fondly. He motioned at the cattle and the ranch house and the buildings far off. "All you see is because of him."

The carriage was almost to them when a head poked out and was pulled back, and a man inside barked an imperious command.

The driver immediately brought the team to a halt.

Fargo's interest perked; that head had been female, and young, and framed by a lustrous mane of corn silk hair. "Who's that?"

The lawman didn't answer.

Two heads filled the windows.

One was the young woman, and closer inspection confirmed she was attractive. Lively green eyes raked Fargo from hat to boots, and full lips curled in a mischievous grin. "What do we have here?"

"Behave yourself, Gwendolyn," the man beside her said. He was older by thirty or forty years, his hair the same color but a lot thinner, his face cragged with lines and his gaze filled with contempt.

"Yes, Father," the young woman said, but she went on ogling Fargo.

"Mr. Stoddard," Marshal Mako said, and touched his hat brim to the woman. "And Miss Stoddard, too."

Horatio Stoddard was staring at Fargo. "Who's this?" he demanded.

"His name is Fargo," Mako said. "He's just passing through."

Gwendolyn frowned. "What a shame."

"Behave, daughter," Horatio warned her. To Fargo he said, "I trust you will find our fair town to your liking."

"I like it already," Fargo replied, devouring the daughter with his eyes.

Horatio looked from her to Fargo and back again. "Yes, well," he said, and scowled. "Just remember we're a law-abiding community." He fixed his gaze on the unconscious form of Carmody Wells. "You caught the fugitive, I see."

"She gave us a good run," Marshal Mako said.

"Foolish," Horatio Stoddard said. "She had to know she couldn't escape. No one ever has."

Just then Carmody raised her head and glared at Stoddard. "Bastard," she spat. "You miserable, rotten son of a bitch."

"You didn't gag her?" Horatio Stoddard said to Mako.

Carmody wasn't done. "You think you're God Almighty, but you're not. You can't get away with this forever. Sooner or later the real law will catch up to you and then it will be you in chains. You and that bitch daughter of yours."

Horatio Stoddard flushed with fury. "Are you just going to sit there?" he snapped at Mako.

The lawman gestured at his deputies. "Gag her, damn it."

Gergan and Clyde swung down. Together, they seized Carmody Wells, who struggled mightily, and hauled her from the horse.

Horatio Stoddard's face lit with a fierce glow. "Be quick about it."

Gwendolyn was amused more than mad. She laughed when Clyde sat on Carmody's legs and Gergan straddled her chest to hold her still.

Gergan patted his pockets and looked up at Marshal Mako. "I don't have anything to gag her with."

"I do!" Gwendolyn squealed in delight. She ducked back into the carriage and reappeared holding a handbag. After a moment's search, she pulled out a lacy pink handkerchief. "Will this do? I don't believe I used it but once."

"Do it," Mako ordered the deputies.

"I'd have to get up to get it," Gergan said. "And Clyde can't hold her down by himself."

"Do I have to do everything?" Mako took the pink handkerchief from Gwendolyn, saying, "Thank you, ma'am." Crumpling it, he tossed it to Gergan.

The skinny deputy gripped Gwendolyn's chin and held it fast. He tried to stuff the handkerchief into her mouth and nearly lost the tips of his fingers. "Behave yourself, woman."

"You're the criminals!" Carmody cried. "All of you. Those badges don't mean a thing."

Gergan tried once more to shove the handkerchief in and she snapped at his hand. Jerking back, he cried, "Ow. The bitch bit me."

Horatio Stoddard puffed his cheeks out in outrage. "Am I surrounded by incompetents? I pinned that badge on you for a reason, Mako. I thought you were the right man for the job. Perhaps I was mistaken."

The marshal turned red. Dismounting, he stepped over to Carmody and placed a hand on one of his six-shooters.

"Unless you want another rap on the noggin, I'd quiet down."

"Go to hell," Carmody screamed. "You're as vile as the rest of them."

Gwendolyn Stoddard laughed.

Marshal Mako shook his head as if in regret. "You've got no more sense than an addlepated goat," he said to his prisoner, and started to draw his revolver.

"No," Fargo said. He said it quietly, yet the marshal and the deputies and the woman froze and looked up at him.

"This is none of your business, mister," Marshal Mako said.

"Why do it the hard way?" Fargo said, climbing down. Walking over to Deputy Gergan, he held out his hand. "The handkerchief."

The tall deputy glanced at Mako. The marshal was clearly puzzled, but he nodded and Gergan gave the pink handkerchief to Fargo.

Carmody Wells was a portrait in perplexity.

"I'm fond of my fingers, so be nice," Fargo said, sinking to a knee. He balled the lacy material and held it poised over her mouth. "Wasn't one bump on your head enough?"

She was still perplexed.

Fargo looked her in the eyes and said, "A pretty girl like you should have more sense."

Surprise registered, and the tension went out of her, and she offered a weary smile. "All right, then," she said. "So long as it's you and not one of these sons of bitches." She opened her mouth wide.

Fargo carefully pressed the gag in. As he removed his hand, he brushed a finger across her upper lip.

Carmody's eyes widened slightly.

"I'll be damned," Deputy Gergan said. "You tamed her right down."

"Didn't he, though?" Deputy Clyde said, and snickered.

"We're obliged," Marshal Mako said.

Fargo stood and smiled. "Anything I can do to help." Turning, he climbed on the Ovaro.

The deputies hoisted Carmody onto Gergan's horse. She was the only one looking at Fargo—and she was the only one who saw him wink.

3

Never, ever in all his wide wanderings, had Skye Fargo come across a town like Fairplay.

It started with the sign. Roughly the size of a buckboard, it was bright green with yellow letters. WELCOME TO FAIR-PLAY, it proclaimed. THE FRIENDLIEST TOWN IN TEXAS. Half of it was taken up by a likeness of the man in the carriage, and under it HORATIO E. STODDARD, FOUNDING FATHER, MAYOR, JUDGE, CIVIC LEADER. Under that, in small print, was NO FIREARMS ARE TO BE WORN OR CARRIED WITHIN THE TOWN LIMITS. NO PUBLIC DRINKING IS ALLOWED EXCEPT IN SALOONS FROM THE HOURS OF NOON UNTIL MID-NIGHT. NO PUBLIC ROWDINESS. NO PUBLIC USE OF PROFAN-ITY. NO SPITTING OF TOBACCO EXCEPT IN SPITTOONS. THE RULE OF LAW WILL PREVAIL.

Fargo had reined up to read it, and when he stopped, so did Marshal Mako, and when Mako stopped, so did the deputies.

"That's some sign," Fargo said.

"Mayor Stoddard's doing," the lawman said. "He's proud of the town he's built."

"No cussing and no spitting?" Fargo marveled.

"Not if you know what's good for you," Deputy Clyde said with another of his snickers.

"Stoddard is a stickler about a few things," Marshal Mako said.

"A few?" Fargo said.

"All he wants is for folks to get along and obey the law," Mako said. "For the town to be the sort of place where people feel safe." He nodded at Fargo's Colt. "The town limits start here, but I'll let you wear that six-gun until we get there. Then you either turn it over to me until you leave or you put it in your saddlebags."

"The people really go around unarmed?"

"Each and every one."

"I must have left Texas and not known it."

Marshal Mako laughed in a good-natured fashion. "What need is there for a six-shooter if no one else is toting one?" He regarded the buildings that were now only a few hundred yards away. "As Mayor Stoddard likes to say, we have a system and it works."

"His system."

"Does it really matter whose? The important thing is that people are safe and happy."

Fargo thought of the men in chains and stripes, digging irrigation ditches and planting crops, and gigged the Ovaro.

"This is my town, too," Marshal Mako remarked, "and I take it personal when anyone causes trouble." He looked at Fargo. "Real personal."

"You said it yourself," Fargo reminded him. "I'm only passing through."

"That's good. Strikes me that you might be too wild and woolly for a place like Fairplay."

"Don't let these buckskins fool you," Fargo said. "I'm civilized as can be."

"Like hell you are," the lawman said. "I can tell about folks. It's not the clothes—it's the man. And you're about as tame as a timber wolf."

"I'm not out to cause trouble."

"You'd better not be," Deputy Clyde said. "We'll have you in leg irons in no time."

Marshal Mako gave him a sharp look. "A person has to be tried and convicted for that to happen."

Clyde snickered. "I ain't seen one yet who hasn't been."

The dirt road turned into Fairplay's main street. The buildings were bright with paint, the windows gleamed clean in the sun. Water troughs were filled, and every board-walk looked to have been swept within the hour. People in good clothes and polished shoes and boots strolled about or conducted business.

"This is about the cleanest town I ever did see," Fargo had to admit.

"Friendly, too," Mako said.

As if to prove him right, smiles were cast at the marshal and his deputies, and hats and derbies were doffed.

"It's friendly, all right," Fargo said. He happened to glance back and noticed that Carmody Wells had raised her head and was giving him a quizzical look.

"This is as far as I go," Mako said, and reined over to a hitch rail. MARSHAL'S OFFICE, read the sign above it. "Don't forget what I told you about your smoke wagon. I wouldn't want to have to arrest you."

"I'll be as peaceable as a puppy," Fargo assured him, and gave Carmody Wells another secret wink.

He rode on down the street. At the first saloon he came to, the Tumbleweed, he unbuckled his gun belt, wrapped the belt around the holster, and placed the Colt in a saddle-bag. He felt half-naked not having it on his hip, but no one else was wearing one, either. There wasn't a single weapon of any kind, anywhere.

The good people of Fairview were trusting sorts, but he wasn't. He left the Arkansas toothpick nestled in its ankle sheath. No one could see it, and he'd be damned if he'd go around unarmed, law or no law.

The whiskey mill's batwings were well-oiled. They didn't creak when he pushed them wide.

Fargo had taken several steps when he stopped and sniffed. Something wasn't right. The place had all the trap-pings of a saloon; there were a long bar and shelves with liquor bottles and tables where cards were being played. But the floor was clean enough to eat off of, and the spittoons were so bright and shiny, they looked as if they'd never been spit in. The smells, too, were different. Most saloons reeked of booze and cigar smoke and sweat. This one was as fragrant as a flower garden in bud.

The barkeep wore a white apron and his beard was neatly trimmed. "How may I help you, sir?"

"You can pinch me so I'll wake up," Fargo said.

The man thought that was worth a chuckle. "I bet it's the clean floor and clean spittoons."

"It's the clean everything," Fargo said. He sniffed loudly a few times. "And what the hell am I smelling?"

"Oh, that," the barkeep said. He pointed at pots of flowers hanging in each corner of the room.

"God Almighty," Fargo said. "Are you loco?"

"It's not my doing," the barman said. "It's the law."

"Every saloon has to have flowerpots?"

The bartender nodded.

"I savvy now," Fargo said. "The whole town is loco."

"It's the mayor," the man said. "He doesn't like stink."

"How's that again?"

"Mayor Stoddard," the barkeep elaborated. "He can't stand what he calls foul odors. So he passed a law that says saloons have to smell nice."

"Maybe I'll pinch my own self," Fargo said.

"That's not all. If you have a horse, be sure and clean up after it."

"You don't mean—?" Fargo didn't finish.

"I do," the bartender said, nodding. "Horse droppings aren't allowed. Or animal droppings of any kind, for that matter. Or didn't you notice how clean the streets are?"

"I *am* still in Texas?"

"Smack in the middle." The man grinned. "Our mayor calls it the wave of the future. The rest of us just call it 'no shit anywhere.'"

"Who did they hire to shovel it all up?"

"They didn't have to hire anyone. That's what the work gangs are for."

"Those men in chains?"

"And the women, too. Our mayor likes to boast that he doesn't favor one gender over the other." The barkeep gazed out the wide front window at the incredibly clean street. "Three times a day they go through with the shit wagon and clean everything up."

"Just when you think you're heard it all."

"I thought the notion was silly, too, at first," the man confided. "But after walking to work a few times and not having to dodge all those piles and puddles, I changed my mind."

"A horse can't piss, either?" Fargo asked in amazement.

"Sure it can," the barkeep said. "So long as whoever owns it spreads dirt over the piss. There are barrels every block or so, with scoops for the dirt."

Fargo recollected seeing a few of the barrels on his way in.

"Don't forget I warned you," the bartender said. "The last thing you want is to have your animal locked away until you pay your fine or serve your time, or both."

Fargo fished out the coins for a bottle and carried it and a glass to an empty table. He hadn't seen any doves, so he was mildly surprised when perfume tingled his nose and a warm hand brushed his neck.

"Care to buy a girl a drink, handsome?"

Calling her a "girl" was a stretch. She had to be thirty or older, but her dress clung to a figure women half her age would have envied. She had eyes as blue as Fargo's and lips a lot redder. Without being invited she sank into a chair across from him and contrived to bend so he got a good look at her abundant cleavage.

"This place is picking up," Fargo said.

"Everyone calls me Jugs on account of—" She stopped

and grinned and motioned at her large breasts. "Well, you can see for yourself."

"Jugs it is." Fargo filled the glass and slid it across.

With a quick gulp, she swallowed every drop.

"Damn," Fargo said. "Go easy on the coffin varnish. I only have the one bottle."

"It's one of my few pleasures these days," Jugs said, "since it's not legal to do the other anymore."

"Which other?"

"Which other do you reckon?" Jugs rejoined, and wriggled seductively in her chair.

To say Fargo was flabbergasted was putting it mildly. "*That's* against the law?"

"Unless you're man and wife," Jugs said. "The town I was at before I came here, I could count on an extra fifty to sixty dollars a week from all the randy goats. But not in Fairplay. If I'm caught, I end up with a chain on my leg."

"Why do you stay?"

Jugs hesitated. "Truth is, I don't miss being poked as much as I thought I would."

"Hell," Fargo said.

"I put in my time here each day and go home at night and sleep like a baby."

"Why do I think you're not being honest with me?"

Jugs glanced about the room and lowered her voice. "Whether I am or I'm not, don't talk so loud. Snooping ears are everywhere."

No one was near enough to overhear them, but Fargo lowered his voice, too. "So you're not against a good poke now and then?"

"Depends. How good a poke are we talking about?"

"It will curl your toes," Fargo boasted.

"Mister," Jugs said, grinning, "come sundown, you're on."

4

Fargo had several hours to kill before nightfall, so he took a stroll around Fairplay. Every street he took, he saw smiling, happy people. Many nodded and acted as friendly as could be.

It made him wonder. People weren't this friendly. Not normally.

It wasn't natural to see so many men walking around unarmed, either. Sure, east of the Mississippi River, it was common. But west of it, and especially in Texas, guns were as commonplace as clothes.

He decided to put the Ovaro up at a stable. The livery attendant was young and freckled and eager to please.

No sooner had Fargo walked back out into the hot sun than he acquired a second shadow.

"You put your animal up for the night?" Deputy Gergan stated the obvious.

"That I did," Fargo said in a much friendlier fashion than he felt.

"The marshal thought you were only staying a few hours," Gergan said.

"Is it against the law to stay the night?"

"Don't be silly. Anyone can come and go however they so please."

"Is there a hotel you'd recommend?"

Gergan waved an arm up the street. "We have a couple

of boardinghouses that put folks up by the night or the month or longer."

"I'm obliged," Fargo said. He turned to go and then turned back as if he'd been struck by a thought. "You're not following me, are you?"

"Why in hell would I do that?" Deputy Gergan asked much too gruffly.

Fargo shrugged. "Just thought it was peculiar, you popping out of nowhere like you did."

"I happened to be passing by."

"You don't say," Fargo said, and let it go at that. He didn't believe it for a second. Apparently Marshal Mako had strangers watched as a matter of course.

"I just did say it," Gergan said.

Fargo smiled. He liked that both deputies were as dumb as tree stumps. It would make it easier. "Give the marshal my regards."

"Sure," Gergan said.

Fargo came to a building with a sign that said they took in boarders, went up onto a porch, and pulled a cord that rang a bell inside. Shortly the door opened, framing an elderly woman with hair as white as snow. "Ma'am," he said.

"I'm Miss Emily. I own this establishment. What can I do for you?"

Fargo explained about needing a room for the night.

"I have one available," Miss Emily said. "You pay in advance and you follow the rules."

"Rules?" Fargo said.

She recited them as if they were the Ten Commandments. "No drinking. No smoking. No tobacco chewing. No women. No loud noises. Lights are to be out by ten. Breakfast is at six. Two eggs, bacon, and toast."

"Sounds like my kind of place," Fargo said.

Miss Emily cocked her head and regarded him as if she

couldn't decide if he was sincere or mocking her. "That's how it is. Stay or not, your choice."

Fargo paid and she ushered him in and down the hall to a room on the right. Small but comfortable, it had a bed and a dresser. Fargo walked over and stared out the window. "All I see is a fence." Not that he gave a damn about the view. With his back to her so she wouldn't notice, he worked the latch.

"What does that matter?" Miss Emily asked.

Fargo faced her and smiled. "It doesn't." He made a show of stretching and patting his stomach. "Where can a gent get a good meal around here? You didn't say a word about supper."

"I only serve breakfast," Miss Emily said. "Try two blocks down and go left. The Cow Bell has good food."

"You're most kind." Fargo laid it on a little thick.

"What I am is practical," Miss Emily said, "and a stickler for the rules."

"There seems to be a lot of that around here," Fargo mentioned.

"And we're better off for it," Miss Emily declared.

She walked him out.

Fargo paused on the front threshold and flicked his eyes right and left.

Down the street, Deputy Gergan ducked into a doorway, but much too slowly.

Grinning, Fargo ambled to the restaurant. The Cow Bell had a damn strange name and, if the aromas were any indication, damn fine food. He ordered a steak with all the trimmings and told the gal in the apron to keep the coffee coming until it leaked out his ears.

About then Deputy Gergan walked past the front window with his hands in his pockets, trying to appear as innocent as the proverbial lamb.

"Let's hear it for simpletons," Fargo said to himself. But it bothered him. He couldn't very well do what he wanted with them watching him so closely.

The meal took his mind off it for a while. Two inches thick and sizzling with juicy fat, the steak made his mouth water. A mountain of mashed potatoes drowned in brown gravy and enough peas to gag a rabbit completed the main course. He also had four slices of bread smeared in butter and coffee.

Fargo wasn't in any hurry. He took so long that Deputy Gergan went past the window twice to make sure he was still in there.

For dessert, Fargo had hot apple pie. When he was done he sat back and patted his stomach again, this time in contentment. He was slightly drowsy, and that wouldn't do. To shake it off, he walked the streets and watched the sun set.

Texas sunsets could be spectacular; this one splashed vivid colors across half the sky.

The first twinkling stars were a reminder to bend his boots to the Tumbleweed. The saloon was crowded. Every table was filled and there was barely elbow space at the bar. Whatever else might be said about the good folks of Fairplay, the men were like men most everywhere else and were fond of their liquor.

Jugs was with a townsman in a bowler. She grinned and nodded at Fargo over the man's shoulder.

Fargo threaded to the far side of the room and stood near a narrow hall that led into the back. He didn't have to wait more than half a minute before Deputy Gergan appeared at the batwings and peered over, trying to spot him.

A single step took Fargo into the hall. He passed a couple of rooms and went out the back door.

Not wasting a second, he headed down a side street. At the third corner he looked back. There was no sign of Gergan.

The heat of the day had given way to the pleasant cool of evening, and a lot of the citizenry were out and about.

Fargo stuck to the shadows. He was the only one in town wearing buckskins, and he'd rather not draw attention.

Half a block from the marshal's office, Fargo turned

into an alley. Once out the other end, he went left past a butcher's.

Ahead, and directly behind the jail, was a long, low building with four small, barred windows. Feeble light filled the squares.

Fargo took a gamble. He looked both ways to be sure no one was around, then ran to the nearest window, rose onto his toes, and peered in.

Small, narrow beds lined both walls. The men were lying back and talking, their faces mirrors of despair. Every last one had a metal strap around his ankle linked by a chain to an iron stanchion in the floor.

Fargo craned his neck to see the only door at the front, then craned it the other way and spied a partition farther down. It only rose half the way to the ceiling, just enough to hide whatever was beyond.

Crouching, Fargo glided to the last of the windows and again rose onto his toes.

Only six beds this time, and only three were occupied. Carmody Wells was on her back with a hand over face, but he recognized her right way.

Another young woman was huddled with an older woman. The young one was small and slim and almost boyish but had a pretty face, and freckles. The older one had gray at the temples and almost as many wrinkles as Miss Emily.

Fargo slid his fingers between the bars and tapped on the glass.

All three women gave a start.

Carmody sat up and looked at the window. Hope lit her face and she slid off the bed and took a step but couldn't take another because of the chain. She said something, but Fargo couldn't hear the words.

A sound from the jail caused Fargo to drop flat. There were voices and the jangle of keys.

A rectangle of light speared the twenty feet of space between the office and the so-called barracks.

In a crouch, Fargo cat-footed to the front.

The marshal's office was well lit, the back door wide open. A desk was visible, and a lamp. No one appeared to be inside.

The door to the barracks was open, and inside someone bellowed, "In your beds! Now! You know what to do, you peckerwoods."

Fargo went to the first window and peered in.

Deputy Clyde and another deputy were overseeing a scramble by the prisoners to turn in.

The new deputy was as big as an ox, with a bushy beard and fists the size of hams. A constant frown creased his craggy face, and he looked ready to tear into anyone who gave him sass.

Clyde was grinning. "Like a bunch of mice," he said, and laughed.

Most of the prisoners couldn't hide their fear. A few glared in defiance.

"Give me cause," the big deputy dared them. "Give me any cause at all."

"You tell them, Brock," Clyde said.

Deputy Brock lumbered down the aisle, a bear spoiling for a fight. "I'd as soon bust your skulls," he declared, "but dead men can't do any work."

Deputy Clyde cackled. "Ain't you a hoot, Brock? You truly are."

Brock stopped at the foot of a bed. The man in it met his stare with surprising calm. "Something on your mind, Harris?"

"Not mine," Harris said. "Only six days to go. I won't do anything to ruin my chances."

Bending, Brock clamped a brawny hand on the man's other leg, midcalf. "Oh?" he said, and his thick fingers tightened.

Harris grimaced and tried to draw away.

"Want to hit me?" Brock taunted. "Want to take a swing?"

"No," Harris got out between clenched teeth. "Never."

"Liar," Brock said, and his fingers seemed to disappear into the folds of Harris's baggy pants. "You know you do. Come on. Just one punch."

"And have to serve another year?" Harris shook his head. "Not on your life."

"There are still six days," Brock said, and let go. Puffing his chest out, he swaggered on to the partition and rapped on the small door. "Knock, knock, ladies," he said. "Ready or not, here we come."

5

Fargo had to see. He made it to the last window and peered in just as Brock and Clyde entered.

The women were in their beds. The older one shrank against the wall, terrified. The pretty young one with the freckles glared in pure and utter hate, not scared at all.

Carmody Jones sat up and said loud enough that Fargo heard her, "Get out of here, you two."

"Shut up, bitch," Deputy Brock said. "We make a bed check every night. You know that."

"Bed check," Deputy Clyde said, and did more of his usual snickering.

Brock moved to Carmody's bunk. He reached out to touch her leg, but she drew it back. "Still got some spunk in you, I see."

"Try that again and you'll find out how much," Carmody said.

"I like 'em feisty." Deputy Brock leered at her. "It's more fun."

"Leave her be," the young woman with the freckles said, "or I'll rip out your throat with my teeth."

Brock laughed. "I'm supposed to be scared of a little thing like you?"

"I won't have this chain on forever," the woman with the freckles said.

"We'll break you like a wild horse," Deputy Brock said, "you and Carmody both."

"Your boss already tried," the freckled woman said. "He's second on my list after that no-good mayor."

"What list?" Brock asked.

"Those I aim to send to hell for how they've treated me."

"Listen to you," Deputy Clyde said in contempt. "We're plumb scared."

"We're tired of your sass," Brock said.

"Do something about it, then," the freckled woman said. "If you're man enough."

Brock stepped to the side of her bunk and reached out to grab her hair, but she swatted his arm away.

Suddenly all of them froze.

Marshal Luther Mako had appeared out of nowhere.

Brock was larger and heavier, but Mako seized his arm and slammed him against the wall so hard, the entire barracks seemed to shake.

"Marshal!" Brock bleated.

Mako placed his hands on his Starr revolvers. "What are you up to?"

"Bed check," Brock said quickly.

Deputy Clyde had stopped snickering and was cringing toward the wall as if in fear of being shot.

"You're never to touch the females," Mako said.

"She was acting up," Deputy Brock said. "And she insulted me."

Just like that, a revolver was in Mako's hand. It was one of the fastest draws Fargo had ever witnessed, and he'd seen more than his share. Mako pressed the muzzle against Brock's cheek and thumbed back the hammer.

"Don't!" Brock bleated. "I was only doing my job."

"Your *job*," Mako said, "is to see that all the prisoners are in their beds."

"I wouldn't have hurt her. I give you my word." Brock opened his mouth to say more but stiffened in fear.

A change had come over Luther Mako. His entire body

seemed to harden, his face most of all, his eyes glittering like twin spikes. Belly or not, here was a man who was as dangerous as any, and then some. In a guttural growl he said, "It must be the wax in your ears."

Brock's throat bobbed. "Wax?"

"When I say to do something, you do it. You don't argue. You don't talk back."

"I'd never," Brock said, and damned if he wasn't trembling.

"You just did. But I'll let you off, this time." Mako stepped back. He twirled his revolver and then reversed the twirl and slid it into its holster as neatly as you please.

"You can depend on me," Brock said. "Honest, you can."

"I hope for your sake you're right," Marshal Mako said.

"I know my job," Brock said.

"Do you? Maybe I'd better set you straight on a few things, anyway." Mako hooked his thumbs in his gun belt. "Mayor Stoddard says how things will be. If he tells you to jump, you ask how high."

"I savvy that," Brock said.

With lightning speed, the six-gun was again in Mako's pudgy hand and pressed against Brock's sweaty face. "Did I say you could talk?"

Brock gulped.

"Go head," Mako said. "I dare you."

Brock tried to shake his head but couldn't with the barrel gouging his cheek.

"If it's not the wax," Mako said, "it must be the empty space between your ears."

Wisely, for once, Brock said nothing.

"So again," Mako said, "if Mayor Stoddard says the women aren't ever to be touched, except by me, then you, by God, better damn well not." He glanced at Deputy Clyde, who cringed as if he'd been slapped. "Isn't that right?"

"Right as rain, Marshal," Clyde squeaked.

"Now, you might think it's strange," Mako went on to Brock, "that the mayor wants us to treat these bitches as if they were ladies—"

"Hey!" Carmody exclaimed.

"—but he's funny that way. He has a great respect for womanhood, as he calls it. That's why he passed a law against whores."

"I always thought that was a shame," Deputy Clyde blurted, and then, appalled by his own boldness, he clamped his mouth shut and put his hand over it.

Mako's jaw muscles twitched. "The point, you jackasses, is that the mayor does everything by the law. His law. Break it and you end up in here. Or worse."

"I won't ever touch them," Brock said. "I promise."

Fargo was so intent on overhearing what was said that he almost failed to notice when Marshal Mako started to turn toward the window. Instantly he ducked and waited for an outcry, but there was none. He didn't tempt fate. He got out of there, counting on the darkness to conceal him if the lawman looked out.

He returned to the saloon by a winding route.

Halfway there, a feeling came over him that he was being followed. He looked back but saw only a man and a woman strolling arm in arm.

Shrugging, Fargo continued on. Half a block later the feeling came over him again. This time he ducked into a dark doorway. Several minutes went by and no one appeared. He stepped out and scanned the street. The few people he saw were going about their own business.

Fargo walked on, puzzled. Normally he could count on his hunches. Honed by his years in the wilds, his instincts were rarely wrong.

The feeling persisted all the way to the Tumbleweed. He glanced over his shoulder as he pushed on the batwings, but again, nothing.

The place was lively. Everyone was having a good time.

The smell of booze, the clink of poker chips, the haze of cigar smoke were a tonic.

Fargo bought a bottle and sat in on a game of poker.

"The usual rules," the dealer informed him as he cut the cards. "Except that you can't ever raise more than a dollar."

Fargo thought his hearing must be going. "Was that your notion of funny?"

"Sure wasn't, mister," another player said. "It's the law."

Fargo absorbed that. "There's a law against betting more than a dollar?"

The dealer nodded. "The mayor says it cuts down on violence."

"That's right," another man said. He favored red suspenders and a green shirt. "Players hardly ever fight over a dollar."

"And everyone goes along with it?"

"It's the law," the dealer said.

A third man mentioned, "If the marshal hears we broke the limit, we'd be hauled off and fined."

"A dollar limit it is," Fargo said.

"It's good you're so reasonable," the dealer said. "Some strangers come riding into Fairplay and reckon they can do as they damn well please."

"They find out soon enough they damn well can't," said the man wearing the red suspenders.

"Are there many sheep raised hereabouts?" Fargo couldn't resist asking.

All the players stared.

"Sheep?" the dealer said.

"This is cow country, mister."

"Woolies wouldn't be welcome here."

"What in hell makes you think there'd be sheep, anyhow?"

Fargo placed his poke on the table and opened it. "Everywhere I go, I hear them."

The man who was about to deal stopped. "I savvy what he's saying, boys. He's saying we're the sheep."

"How come us?" the man in the suspenders said.

"You'd better be careful with talk like that, mister," the dealer warned. "Some of us might not take too kindly to it."

"What will you do besides twiddle your thumbs?" Fargo wondered.

"Insult us all you want," the dealer said. "We like a peaceful town."

"Everyone's happy here," the man with the suspenders said.

Fargo knew he should keep his mouth shut, but he couldn't. "Except the ones in chains."

"They brought it on themselves. They broke the law."

"What concern is it of yours, anyhow?" the last player demanded.

"None," Fargo said. "In a day or two your town will be miles behind me." He almost added, "And good riddance."

"Fine by us," the dealer said. "We don't cotton to folks who don't cotton to us."

The game got under way. Fargo ignored their glares and frowns. To spite them he always raised the dollar limit. After an hour he was six dollars ahead. At that rate, in a hundred years he'd be rich.

A clock over the bar pegged the time at fifteen minutes to midnight when Fargo announced he needed to turn in. He had half a bottle left and took it with him.

The night air was invigorating.

Going around to the side of the saloon, he scanned the street, then moved to the rear.

Jugs was true to her word; it wasn't long before she stepped out the back door with a shawl over her shoulder. Coming into the shadows, she grinned.

"Ready for some fun, handsome?"

"I was born ready," Fargo said.

6

Initially Fargo had intended to use his room. It was why he undid the latch, so she could sneak in through the window. But Jugs wanted to use hers.

No sooner had she closed the door and thrown the bolt than she pressed herself to him with a fierce hunger.

"I've been thinking about you all night," Jugs said when they broke for breath.

"You're taking a chance," Fargo reminded her. The last thing he wanted was to get her into trouble with the town's outrageous excuse for the law.

"I don't care. It's been too damn long. I want it. I *need* it."

Fargo cupped her bottom and she squirmed in delight. "I won't tell if you don't."

Jugs started to laugh, and caught herself. "We have to be quiet about it," she said with a nervous glance at the door. "The walls aren't that thick and the couple who owns the place likes to snoop."

"We could ride out of town," Fargo suggested. "Find a grassy spot." He didn't need a bed to do the deed.

Jugs shook her head. "Anyone who saw us leaving at this time of night might be suspicious and report us to the marshal. I'm pretty well known, thanks to all the men who come into the saloon. Their wives don't like me one bit."

"Why in hell do you stay?"

"Like I told you before, the work is easy and I don't mind not having the other as much as I thought I would."

Jugs grinned and nipped his chin with her teeth. "Now and then, though, I just have to."

"So you keep saying. But words are cheap."

"Big man, I'll show you a lot more than words," Jugs teased.

And with that, her mouth was on his. She inhaled his tongue as her fingers pried at his belt buckle with an urgency that wouldn't be denied.

She removed his hat and his bandanna, then pushed him toward the bed with one hand while working at her dress with the other.

"I will drain you dry," Jugs breathlessly promised, flush with desire.

"I'll believe it when I feel it," Fargo said.

Grinning, Jugs pushed him onto the bed, climbed on, and straddled him. She had undone a dozen of her buttons and commenced to peel out of her dress with an alacrity born of experience.

Fargo reached up to help and she playfully swatted his hand.

"Put them to better use," Jugs scolded.

Fargo did. He hiked her chemise and pressed his palms to nipples as hard as tacks. She arched her back and gasped. He pinched and pulled, eliciting a moan.

As he went on kneading, she closed her eyes and tilted her head back.

"Yes," she whispered. "Oh yesssss."

Fargo believed her claim that she hadn't done it in a while. She wanted him, wanted him badly, and she wasted no time in sliding his buckskin shirt over his head and tossing it to the floor.

"All these muscles," Jugs said in awe as she ran her fingers over his chest and the washboard knots that were his stomach. "I had no idea."

"Like them, do you?"

"Love them," Jugs said throatily, and to prove it, she

bent and lavished hot, wet kisses from his shoulders to his hips.

Fargo grew hot all over. He got her dress off and added it to the growing pile. The chemise she slid off herself.

Finally Jugs was naked.

He drank in her charms: her full, round breasts, her flat belly, the triangle of her bush, and creamy thighs that went on forever.

"Like what you see?" she teased back.

"Love it." Fargo mimicked her.

They caressed and stroked and kissed.

Fargo lost all sense of time, all sense of everything, save the heady sensual sensations she provoked. And Lordy, she was good at provoking them.

Experience, folks liked to say, was the best teacher. Judging by her performance, Jugs had more experience than most ten women. She knew just what to do to bring him to a fever pitch. Each time she brought him down again before he exploded. She was a master at prolonging their mutual pleasure.

Fargo didn't mind. He had all night. Or most of it.

Jugs stayed on top of him. She seemed to like that. It was her, not him, who fed his manhood into her velvet sheath. When he was all the way in, she became perfectly still for all of a minute, her full lips spread in a smile of utter contentment. "You feel so good, handsome. You have no idea."

"Less talk and more fucking," Fargo said.

Jugs laughed lightly, and got down to it. In rising excitement she pumped and pumped.

Fargo fondled her mounds and her thighs and wherever else he could reach while she licked and bit his neck and stuck the tip of her tongue in his ear.

Her gush preceded his. The bed shook but didn't thump and neither of them cried out. She did open her mouth as if she was going to scream, but the only sound she made was a tiny mew.

Then it was his turn.

Afterward, Jugs lay on his chest and played with his hair. "Give me a minute and I'll be raring to go again."

"A whole minute?"

Jugs giggled and nuzzled his throat. "How many helpings am I allowed?"

"As many as you want."

She wanted three. The last took the longest. They built to it slowly and when the flood was over she collapsed and closed her eyes and was out to the world.

Fargo was drowsy, himself. He eased her onto her side, stretched out, and drifted off. He hoped he wouldn't oversleep. His habit was to wake at the crack of dawn; today he wanted to be up earlier.

Fate smiled on him. A barking dog woke him a full hour before daybreak. He slipped out of bed and dressed without disturbing her.

The boardinghouse was quiet. So was the town. The dog had stopped yapping after an angry shout, presumably from its owner.

Fargo wondered if barking dogs were against the law, too.

Hardly anyone was out and about. A milk wagon clattered down the main street, the driver half dozing in the seat.

A block over, hooves thudded and faded.

Soon Fargo was where he wanted to be, a recessed doorway that gave him a good vantage of the barracks.

Not until a rosy blush touched the eastern sky did sounds come from the marshal's office. The back door opened and out shuffled Deputy Brock, scratching himself. He carried a set of keys. Yawning, he had to try twice to open the padlock on the barracks door. "Rise and shine, you miserable bastards," he hollered. "You know the routine." He closed the door but didn't lock it and went back into the marshal's office.

The barred windows lit with light. There was coughing, and voices, and someone sobbed.

About ten minutes went by and Deputy Brock reappeared. Deputy Gergan was with him, toting a rifle. They went into the barracks and after a lot of yelling and cussing, Gergan reappeared and moved to one side.

Their chains rattling and clanking, the prisoners filed out. The sixteen men first, the three women after. Their clothes needed washing. So, for that matter, did they.

Deputy Brock snarled for them to halt and they stood still as he went down the line, checking that their leg irons were secure. He leered at Carmody and she stared at him as if he were a disease.

The young woman with the freckles had her fists balled and looked ready to tear into him if he gave her cause.

Out of the office strode Marshal Luther Mako, trailed by Deputy Clyde.

"Morning," the lawman said.

None of the convicts responded.

"We're splitting you up like we did yesterday," Mako announced. "Some of you will work on the irrigation ditches, some of you on the planting."

A man muttered something.

"I didn't catch that, Thomas," Marshal Mako said. "What did you say?"

Thomas shook his head.

"I won't ask you again."

"I said," the man angrily replied, "another day in hell."

"Who's to blame for that? You're the one who was caught stealing."

"We both know the truth," Thomas said bitterly.

"Which is?"

"No, you don't," Thomas said. "I'm not saying anything that will add to my sentence."

"You shouldn't say anything at all," the lawman said. "What's the rule?"

"No," Thomas said. "Don't."

"What's the rule?" Mako asked again.

"We're not," Thomas said, and gulped, "we're not to speak unless spoken to."

"Yet you did."

"Please, no."

"Add another week," Marshal Mako said. "I'll have to clear it with the mayor, but I reckon he'll agree."

Thomas tried to move toward him and was stopped by the chain. "Damn you to hell! How can you do this to people?"

"Two weeks," Mako said.

"Bastard," Thomas cried, shaking a fist. "I've had it—do you hear me?"

"Tom, don't!" Carmody Wells yelled.

Deputy Brock started forward but stopped when Marshal Mako gestured.

"Let him speak his piece."

"You're damn right I will!" Thomas said, his voice cracking. "You're crooked, the whole bunch of you. You trump up charges. You run sham trials."

"You were caught red-handed," the lawman said.

"I never laid eyes on that money before your deputy pulled it from my saddlebags," Thomas said, glaring at Deputy Clyde.

"So you say," Marshal Mako said.

"You're scum. Vermin through and through." Thomas laughed a near-hysterical laugh. "Do you know the only difference between you and a cockroach?" He didn't wait for an answer. "Cockroaches don't wear tin stars."

Marshal Mako smiled slowly. He slowly walked over to Thomas, and nodded slowly. "You're right. Two weeks wouldn't be fair. But a broken nose would."

"What?"

The lawman's hand blurred. The heavy *thwack* of the revolver barrel brought a spurt of scarlet.

Thomas shrieked and folded, his hands over his face.

Mako wasn't finished. His revolver rose once, twice, three times. Then he calmly wiped his revolver on Thomas's shirt. "Take him back inside. He's to spend the day chained in his bunk. No food, no water. You hear me?"

Fargo had seen enough. He got out of there. If he'd had any doubts before, he had none now.

He was about to stick his head in a bear's mouth and hoped to hell it didn't get bit off.

7

Fargo slept until noon. He would have slept longer, but some kids playing and shouting woke him and he couldn't get back to sleep. Reluctantly he got out of bed. He filled the china washbasin with water from a pitcher and washed up. He dressed and opened his door and stopped short. "Miss Emily?"

The old woman stood there with her hands on her thin hips and accusation in her eyes. "You didn't come back last night."

"So?" Fargo said.

"You paid for a room, but you didn't use it. I find that peculiar." Miss Emily waited, and when Fargo didn't say anything, she went on. "I happen to know for a fact that you straggled in about six o'clock this morning."

"Sounds about right," Fargo said.

"Where were you?"

Controlling his temper, Fargo replied, "I don't see where that's any of your business, ma'am."

"A person pays for a room, usually he uses it."

"Usually," Fargo said.

Miss Emily jabbed a finger at him. "I think you were up to no good. And we don't abide shenanigans in Fairplay. Not at all."

"It's some town."

"You don't like us. I can tell. But that's all right. I don't

40

like you much, either." Miss Emily shot him a glance of disapproval and walked off.

Great way to start the day, Fargo reflected, and ambled outside. The glare of the summer sun caused him to pull his hat brim low.

His stomach growled, so he made his way to the Tumbleweed for his breakfast. "A bottle of Monongahela," he told the bartender.

At that hour few of the tables were taken. He was pouring his first glass when in came Deputy Clyde, who did a strange thing.

Clyde saw him, stopped dead in his tracks, smiled slyly, and wheeled and walked back out.

"What the hell?" Fargo said. He tossed off the drink and gave a slight shake as the whiskey took effect.

Miss Emily was right. He didn't like Fairplay. In all his travels, there had been few towns he liked less. It was a nest of vipers, and the hell of it was, the vipers ran things.

Rather than sit there, Fargo decided to check on the Ovaro. He took the bottle and pushed on the batwings.

"Watch it," a sultry voice snapped. "You almost hit me in the face."

Fargo peered over. "Well, now," he said. "The day is looking up."

"I beg your pardon?" Gwendolyn Stoddard said. She was dressed in finery that would have drawn stares in Kansas City or St. Louis, including a pink parasol.

Fargo stepped out. "The lady from the carriage," he said.

Gwendolyn looked him up and down, and her face softened. "Mr. Fargo. I remember you from yesterday," she said.

"I recollect those lips of yours."

Gwendolyn gave a throaty laugh. "Aren't you the bold devil? Most men hereabouts are too afraid to even speak to me."

"You bite their heads off?"

"My father might."

"Fairplay's illustrious mayor," Fargo said. "And most everything else."

Gwendolyn twirled her parasol. "You'd better not let him hear you say that. He wouldn't like it even a little bit."

"Ask me if I give a good damn."

Gwen studied him. "Is it that you're braver than most or that you have no brains?"

"I'll let you decide."

"You interest me, Mr. Fargo," Gwendolyn said. "Walk with me a spell." It was a command. She sashayed past, her perfume enough to entice a monk.

Fargo fell into step. "What do you want to talk about?"

"You," Gwendolyn said. "My father thinks you're a troublemaker. He says he could see it in your eyes."

"I'm as law-abiding as the next gent," Fargo said.

"I hope so. Father asked the marshal to keep an eye on you."

"Did he, now?" Fargo said. That explained the deputies following him around.

"You'd be wise to be on your best behavior."

Fargo saw that people were quick to get out of her way and more than a few cast fearful glances. "I always am," he lied.

Gwen did more twirling. "My father isn't to be trifled with. He likes to control those around him, and he can be mean when he's crossed."

"You don't say."

"I'm an adult, as anyone can plainly see," Gwen continued as if she hadn't heard him. "Yet he treats me as if I'm still his little girl. I can't stand that."

"Poor you."

Gwendolyn stopped. "Are you being smart with me?"

"I saw your house, your carriage," Fargo said. "You have it better than most."

"I can't help it my father has money. Not that he cares that he does."

"A rich man who doesn't care that he's rich?"

"Money is like everything else to my father. A means to an end."

"What end?" Fargo was curious enough to ask.

"Power." Gwendolyn said the word in the way a parson might say "God." "My father craves it more than anything. The power to do as he pleases. The power to make others do as he pleases."

"I'm surprised you'd admit it."

"Why wouldn't I? We all have our abiding passions, you might call them. My father's is power." Her eyes narrowed. "What's yours? I wonder."

"I like to see what's over the next horizon," Fargo confessed.

"Wanderlust? *That's* your passion?"

Fargo ran his gaze from her lustrous hair to the tips of her new shoes. "I have others."

Gwendolyn coyly raised the parasol so only her twinkling eyes showed. "Aren't you the wolf in buckskins?"

"Would you like to hear me howl?"

She gave him the same lustful scrutiny he'd given her. "You tempt me. You truly do."

"I have a room."

Gwendolyn stopped and lowered the parasol, her mouth agape. "*Now?* Why, it's not even the middle of the afternoon."

"That matters?"

"You bet it does. Someone might see us."

"And you're worried word will get to your pa."

"You're damn right I am," Gwendolyn declared. "You don't know him like I do. He expects me to be a prim and proper lady. I dare show an interest in a man and he calls me a hussy."

"What does he call you if you let one poke you?"

"You needn't be so blunt about it," Gwendolyn said. "But to answer your question, he'd disown me and hang me out to dry."

Fargo felt little sympathy. He had a feeling she pretty much got whatever she wanted. The signs were all there; she was as spoiled as they came.

They neared the general store just as two men strolled out.

Gwendolyn abruptly halted. "Oh God. Not them. Not now."

Her father had on the best clothes a lot of money could buy. He was smiling, but his smile faded and was replaced by anger.

Marshal Mako had been listening to something the ruler of Fairplay's roost was saying. He didn't look happy to see Fargo and the girl together, either.

"What's this, daughter?" Horatio Stoddard said. "I leave you alone for half an hour and who do you take up with?"

"It's not what you think, Father," Gwendolyn said archly. "We've barely passed the time of day."

"What are you doing with my daughter?" the mayor demanded.

"She was telling me how much she adores you," Fargo said.

"She what?"

Fargo nodded. "She wouldn't stop jabbering about how you're the kindest, nicest, most considerate hombre who ever lived."

"Are you pulling my leg?"

"I'm pulling something," Fargo said.

Marshal Mako shifted his pudgy hands close to his pistols. "You'll treat His Honor with respect."

Fargo knew he shouldn't, but he said, "I would if I had any."

Horatio Stoddard sniffed. "I don't think I like you very much, young man."

"I'll try not to lose sleep over it."

Gwen appeared shocked that anyone would dare talk to her father that way. "Please," she said. "Don't be mean. He doesn't like it when people are mean."

"Has he looked in a mirror lately?" Fargo said.

"*Enough*," Marshal Mako barked.

To Fargo's surprise, Horatio Stoddard smiled and motioned. "That's all right, Luther. Let him have his fun. It's good to know where he stands on things."

Fargo had said too much already. But just being near the man was enough to make him want to kick his teeth in. "How about if I go my way and you go yours?" He touched his hat brim to Gwen and headed across the street. Once on the other side, he looked back.

The mayor and the marshal were glaring.

Gwendolyn was twirling her parasol and distinctly unhappy.

"That was dumb," Fargo said to himself. He continued on to the stable. He'd only intended to check on the Ovaro, but now he threw his saddle blanket and saddle on and rode out of town along the road he had entered by.

It wasn't long before he came on the men in stripes, digging another irrigation ditch.

The same wagon was parked at the side of the road, and the same stubby driver with a shotgun was perched on the seat.

Drawing rein, Fargo said, "Afternoon. Who might you be?"

"Go away," the man said. To stress his point, he pointed the shotgun.

"Not very friendly, are you?"

"Not even a little bit."

Fargo kept riding. At the turnoff to the ranch house, he saw more stripes; several men were planting in the mayor's garden.

He didn't see the women anywhere. Which was unfortunate. He'd like to let Carmody Wells know what he was up to.

After his little run-in with His Honor, he was more determined than ever to go through with it.

Even if it got him killed.

8

Jugs wasn't at the Tumbleweed. The bartender told Fargo she hadn't shown up for work, and mentioned how she'd never done that before. Yes, the barman had sent someone to her room, but she wasn't there.

Fargo sat in on a poker game. Despite the stupid limit, over the next hour he added eleven dollars to his poke.

Jugs still hadn't shown up.

Fargo claimed a corner chair and pondered. Come daybreak, he planned to have the Ovaro and a horse for Carmody Wells hid in an alley near the barracks. When the deputies came to wake the prisoners for another day of forced labor, they were in for a surprise. He'd take the keys at gunpoint, free those poor bastards and the women, help Carmody on the horse, and get the hell out of Fairplay.

It sounded simple enough. But all sorts of things could go wrong. The worst would be if Marshal Mako took part. He'd seen Mako draw. The man was greased lightning.

Fargo realized he might be making a fool of himself. He hardly knew Carmody Wells. But he'd be damned if he'd just ride off and leave her to be pistol-whipped and suffer whatever other abuse the lawmen heaped on her.

What he'd like to do—what he'd *really* like to do—was beat Horatio Stoddard to a pulp. The mayor was the cause of all this. Him and his high-handed ways. Imposing laws that no other town in Texas would stand for.

That said something about the people of Fairplay. It wasn't right to call them "people."

They were sheep. They'd rather be lorded over than stand up for themselves. They had no gumption. No grit. That, and they actually liked being told what to do so they could go about their little lives in peace.

They'd rather be controlled than live as free men and women.

Fargo had never seen the like. Not to this degree. Not west of the Mississippi River.

Back east, there were towns galore where no one was allowed to wear a gun and gambling was outlawed and ladies of the night weren't allowed to parade their wares.

Things that, to Fargo, made life worth living.

The chiming of a clock on a shelf behind the bar brought him out of himself. It was ten o'clock. Early for him to turn in, but he had a busy day tomorrow.

The night air felt good as he strolled to Miss Emily's boardinghouse. He was surprised when the front door opened as he reached for it and Miss Emily stood there with the most peculiar smile.

"Look who it is," she said.

"I'd like the same room for another night," Fargo said.

"Would you, now?"

"Can I or can't I?"

"By all means. But I can't say I'll be sorry to see you go. You're rude, for one thing. For another, it's those eyes of yours."

"My eyes?" Fargo didn't understand.

"They look down on us. As if you're better than we are."

Fargo tried to remember if he'd ever looked at her that way.

"You ride in here with your smug airs and go around doing as you please."

"Do I?"

"Our laws are precious to us. They preserve the peace, and that's what counts."

"Can I go to the room or do you aim to blather me to death?"

Miss Emily reddened. "You think we're stupid, but we're not. You'll find that out."

"I won't be sticking around that long."

Her peculiar smile returned. "Is that a fact?" Miss Emily tittered and put her back to a wall so he could walk past. "Have a good rest," she said sweetly.

Damned biddy, Fargo thought. He made sure to bolt his door so she couldn't poke her head in. He took off his hat and set it on the dresser and stretched out fully clothed on the bed, his boots over the end board so his spurs didn't tear the quilt. He wouldn't have time in the morning to wash up and dress.

He stifled a yawn.

Closing his eyes, Fargo thought about the woman he was about to risk his hide to help. He thought about the look she'd given him, that desperate look of despair and appeal. It could be she had a beau somewhere. He might go to all this trouble for a peck on the cheek or a handshake, and off she'd ride.

Soon he drifted off. He couldn't have been asleep more than half an hour when there was a light knock on his door.

"Mr. Fargo?" Miss Emily called.

"I'm in bed," Fargo said, annoyed that she had woke him.

"May I speak with you, please?"

"Tomorrow," Fargo said. He'd had enough of her scorn for one night.

"It's important. It involves a young woman by the name of Jugs."

That brought Fargo to his feet. He went to the door and threw it open. "What about—" he began, and got not further.

Two revolver muzzles blossomed in his face. One was held by Deputy Gergan to the right of the doorway, the other by Deputy Clyde on the left.

In the middle, next to a beaming Miss Emily, stood Marshal Luther Mako.

49

"What's this?" Fargo demanded.

"As if you don't know," Miss Emily said.

"We're obliged for you helping us," Marshal Mako said to her. "You can go now."

Miss Emily kept on beaming contemptuously at Fargo. "Now you'll get yours. You and your rude ways."

"I said to go," Marshal Mako said.

"Think you're better than most folks," Miss Emily went on.

"For the last time," Mako said sternly, and put a hand on her arm.

"I'll go. But it does my heart good to see him get his comeuppance."

"Yes, ma'am," Mako said, and started her down the hall. "Stay out of the way in case he resists arrest."

"Arrest?" Fargo said.

Deputy Clyde snickered.

Fargo glared at him and Clyde withered and firmed his grip on his six-shooter.

As for Mako, he squared around and said in a formal tone, "Skye Fargo, by the authority invested in me by the town of Fairplay, I hereby take you into custody."

"The hell you say," Fargo said.

"How come you have to use those fancy words when you do it?" Deputy Gergan said to Mako.

"The mayor's doing," the lawman replied. "Now shut up." Gergan blanched.

"As for you," Mako said to Fargo, "I'd advise you to come along quiet-like. You'll be taken to the jail and held there until the trial."

"What's the charge?"

"Charges," Marshal Mako corrected him.

"This should be good," Fargo said.

The lawman recited them. "You violated town ordinance by sleeping with a prostitute. You violated another by carrying a whiskey bottle on a public street. You violated a third by making unwanted advances on another woman. Lewd conduct, the mayor calls that."

"He would," Fargo said. "Who was the woman?" As if he couldn't guess.

"You'll hear all about it at the trial." Mako placed his hands on his Starr revolvers. "Step out here with your hands in front of you. Try anything, and we'll gun you."

Fargo believed him. As much as he resented it, he did as they wanted, and inwardly winced when handcuffs were quickly placed on his wrists. "I'll remember this," he said.

"You'll have more to remember real soon," Marshal Mako said, taking him by the elbow.

"So this is how you do it," Fargo said.

"Let's go."

"And you can sleep at night?"

"I wouldn't goad me, were I you. I'm just doing my job."

"Is that what you call having your nose buried up Stoddard's ass?"

Pain exploded in Fargo's head. His knees folded and he fell hard to the floor and for a few moments he thought he would pass out.

"I warned you," Marshal Mako said, twirling a revolver into its holster. "I won't take guff."

Both deputies laughed.

Gritting his teeth against the agony, Fargo growled, "Try that when I'm not in cuffs."

"On your feet." Marshal Mako grabbed hold of the back of his shirt, hauled him up, and pushed.

Fargo stumbled and almost fell. Getting his balance, he saw Miss Emily holding the front door open and grinning in delight.

"You got yours," she said happily.

"Bitch."

"You have a filthy tongue."

"Don't worry. I'd never stick it up you."

Miss Emily hissed and kicked him in the shin.

"None of that," Marshal Mako said. He pushed Fargo harder. "Keep going. You know the way to the jail."

"You'll get yours, too," Fargo said.

"Was that a threat? We can add another charge if you want."

"Go to hell."

"Threatening a lawman it is, then."

Fargo knew better, but he was so mad that the words were out of his mouth before he could stop himself. "Does your mother know she gave birth to a son of a bitch?"

The second blow was harder than the first.

Fargo was vaguely aware of falling and then of being dragged by the arms by the deputies.

"He sure is a heavy cuss," Deputy Clyde complained.

"He talks tough," Deputy Gergan said, "but he won't after the mayor gets through with him."

Struggling to stay conscious, Fargo felt his knees and boots scraping the street and then they were in the marshal's office and he was dumped on a wooden floor.

"Do we put him in the barracks with the rest?" Deputy Gergan asked.

"Not until after the trial," Marshal Mako said. "For now we hold him in a cell."

Fargo was dragged again, and flung, and heard a sound that most men dreaded: the loud metallic clang of a cell door slamming shut.

9

It took hours for Fargo's head to stop hurting. He lay on the cell bunk, stewing.

He'd intended to spirit Carmody Wells away, and that was all. Now it was different. Now it was personal.

He'd do a lot more than free her before he was through.

Marshal Mako left after half an hour. So did Deputy Clyde.

Gergan sat at a desk reading or dozing until he was relieved about midnight by Brock.

The big deputy closed and bolted the front door and came over to the cell.

"So you're the hombre who got on the mayor's bad side?"

"Is that a fact?" Fargo said.

"Mister, he plumb hates you." Brock grinned and winked. "I hear tell it has something to do with that daughter of his taking a shine to you."

Fargo grunted.

"You're taking it awful calm," Deputy Brock said. "Or don't you know he could sentence you to a year or more at hard labor for what you've done?"

"He thinks so," Fargo said.

"You'd better get it through your head that Mayor Stoddard is the next thing to God around here. What he wants, he gets."

"One of these days he'll get more than he bargained for."

"Listen to you." Brock laughed. "Haven't you seen the prisoners out in the barracks? You'll be there before too long, wearing a chain just like they do. That will take you down a peg."

"What about my horse?" Fargo thought to ask.

"It's at the livery, I was told. It'll stay there until after the trial. Likely as not, the mayor will put it up for sale to defray the costs of your incarceration, as he likes to say. Or maybe he'll keep it for himself."

"Over my dead body."

"That can be arranged, too," Deputy Brock said, and turned. "You go to court at nine in the morning, by the way."

"That quick," Fargo said.

"The mayor doesn't let grass grow under him when it comes to new workers."

The deputy lumbered off.

Fargo continued to fume. Making sure that Brock wasn't watching, he slipped his hand into his boot and reassured himself the Arkansas toothpick was snug in its ankle sheath. They'd frisked him and taken his poke and bandanna, but they hadn't searched his boots.

Their carelessness would cost them.

For now, there was nothing Fargo could do except bubble with impatience as the night crawled on turtle's feet. His sleep was fitful. When a rooster crowed to herald the new dawn, he felt as if he'd barely slept a wink.

Marshal Mako showed up at six. The deputies went through the morning routine with the prisoners in the barracks, and the wagon departed.

Only then did Mako come over. "Your trial is today."

"So I heard."

"Act up in court and it will go hard for you," Mako warned.

"It's going to go hard for somebody," Fargo said.

"There you go again. That mouth of yours will get you five years if you're not careful."

Deputy Clyde brought a bowl of oatmeal and a glass of milk, but Fargo didn't touch either.

"Any chance of getting some whiskey?"

Clyde tittered and shook his head in amusement. "You're a regular hoot."

At a quarter to nine, Marshal Mako stepped to the gun rack and armed himself with a short-barreled shotgun. He passed out one to Gergan and one to Clyde.

It was Gergan who unlocked the cell.

"Nice and easy does it," Marshal Mako said. "You don't want to give us an excuse."

Fargo strode out. He wasn't in the best of moods. In addition to everything else, his head had a dull ache and his wrists were chafed from having the cuffs on all night. "Can't say much for your hospitality."

"Flap your gums while you can," Mako said. "Once you're sentenced, you don't get to speak unless you're spoken to."

Fairplay didn't have a courthouse. Trials were conducted in a side room off the mayor's office.

Fargo was made to sit on a long benched flanked by the deputies. He was surprised to see Jugs there. He noticed a bruise on her left cheek and another on her chin. She avoided meeting his gaze.

A court clerk went through the usual rigmarole, and Mayor Horatio Stoddard, wearing a long robe and carrying a sheath of papers, grandly entered like a king about to hold court. He perched in his high seat and smiled down at them. Picking up a gavel, he rapped it several times while declaring, "Court is now in session. Let the proceedings commence."

"Don't I get a lawyer?" Fargo asked.

About to consult his papers, Stoddard looked up in annoyance. "Eh? What was that? You're requesting the services of a counsel?"

"Why not?" Fargo said.

"Do you have the money to hire one?"

"Ask your tin star. He has my poke."

Stoddard turned to the marshal. "Is this true, Marshal Mako?"

"No, Your Honor. We searched him when we arrested him. He didn't have a cent to his name."

Fargo wondered what they were up to and found out when the mayor nodded as if he suspected as much and said, "We'll add vagrancy to the charges already lodged against him. That's good for another six months."

"If I'm found guilty," Fargo said.

"If you're—?" Stoddard said, and smothered a laugh. "Yes, indeed. We must adhere to the letter of the law, mustn't we?"

"You wouldn't know the letter of the law," Fargo said, "if it bit you on the ass."

Deputy Gergan hiked his shotgun as if to bash Fargo in the face.

"No!" Stoddard barked. "No violence, if you please." Placing his hands flat, he bent forward. "I will only warn the defendant this once. Proper decorum will be followed at all times."

"I can't say 'ass'?" Fargo said.

"You may not insult the integrity of this court in any manner," Stoddard replied.

"It doesn't have any."

Stoddard sat back and scowled. "Enough. If the defendant persists, you are to gag him, Marshal Mako. Is that understood?"

"Yes, sir," the lawman answered.

"Now, then. Where were we?" Stoddard said.

"Vagrancy," Fargo reminded him.

"Ah yes." Stoddard consulted a paper. "You are hereby charged with that, as well as threatening an officer of the law, consorting in proscribed carnal activities, and obstruction of justice. How does the defendant plead?"

"Proscribed?" Fargo said.

"That means illegal," Stoddard said.

"It's against the law to fuck?"

Deputy Clyde laughed and drew a glare from Marshal Mako.

"It's against the law to solicit the services of a prostitute," Stoddard said.

"I didn't solicit anything," Fargo said. "She wanted to hump me."

"Oh, really?" Stoddard turned toward Jugs. "Miss Bedelia Cavendish, will you rise, please, and step to the witness stand, where the bailiff will swear you in?"

Jugs, her chin bowed, obeyed.

Fargo could imagine what was coming. This bunch didn't miss a trick.

"Now, then," Stoddard began, "you just heard the defendant. I will ask you point-blank. Is he telling the truth?"

Jugs glanced nervously at Marshal Mako, then said so quietly it was hard to hear her, "No, Your Honor."

"Tell us in your own words what occurred."

Jugs swallowed and had to try twice before she got out, "I was working at the Tumbleweed when"—she stopped and trembled—"when this gentleman came up to me and asked me if I'd go to bed with him for, uh, forty dollars."

"Aha!" Stoddard exclaimed. "And did you agree?"

Jugs glanced at Mako again. "To my shame, Your Honor, I did."

"Very well. That will be all."

"I can go?"

"The marshal has informed me that you agreed to testify in exchange for immunity from prosecution. So yes, you're free to depart."

Jugs gave Fargo a look that said she was sorry more eloquently than if she'd said it out loud. With a swish of her dress, she whisked out of there.

"As the defendant just heard," Stoddard said, "his lie has been exposed."

"It's her word against mine," Fargo said.

"This court prefers to believe her."

"I'm shocked."

Stoddard picked up the gavel. "Have you anything more to say before sentence is pronounced?"

Fargo sat up. "That's it?"

"We believe in a speedy trial."

"I don't get to take the stand? Or call witnesses of my own?"

"What good would that do? We've heard the prostitute and we have Marshal Mako's written testimony. That's all this court requires."

"You mealymouthed sack of shit."

Horatio Stoddard became the same color as a beet. With a sharp gesture, he growled, "I've listened to enough. Marshal, gag the prisoner."

"Before you do," Fargo quickly said, "you'd better decide what to do about the army."

Mako paused in the act of taking a crumpled handkerchief from a vest pocket, while Stoddard scrunched his face in confusion.

"The what?"

"The army," Fargo repeated.

"What can they possibly have to do with this?"

Fargo touched his cuffed hands to his chest. "In case no one told you, I scout for a living."

"So?"

"So I'm due at Fort Bowie by the end of the month."

"So?"

"So they knew I was coming this way. When I don't show up"—Fargo shrugged—"could be they'll send someone to look for me."

It was called grasping at a straw. He waited to see what effect his bald-faced lie would have.

10

Horatio Stoddard straightened and sat back. His eyebrows tried to meet over his nose. "You expect the court to believe that?"

Fargo shrugged and said as casually as he could, "If you can't tell what I do for a living, you're dumber than a stump."

Marshal Mako cleared his throat. "He did say he was a scout when we first met."

"He sure looks like one," Deputy Gergan threw in.

"Daniel Boones," Deputy Clyde added. "Why can't they wear clothes like everybody else?"

Stoddard drummed his fingers and crooked one at the marshal. "A word, if you please. Approach the bench."

Fargo tried to hear what they said, but they whispered. Stoddard appeared agitated. When Marshal Mako came back he didn't look happy.

"There will be a delay in sentencing," Stoddard announced, "while this issue of the army is resolved. The defendant will be held in jail until such time as the court deems otherwise."

"On your feet," Mako said to Fargo. "Boys, cover him."

Fargo was elated. He'd bought some time. But how much? As they marched him from the municipal building, he asked, "What did he mean by resolved?"

"The mayor knows a few people in high places," Marshal Mako said. "He's going to check on your story. He's writing a letter to a colonel he knows. We should hear back in a couple of weeks, maybe a little longer."

"In the meantime I rot behind bars?"

"I'll find ways to keep you busy," Mako said.

Fargo spotted Jugs. She was across the street, staring sadly. He smiled to show there were no hard feelings, but he couldn't tell if she noticed.

"Just so you know," Marshal Mako said. "If it turns out you're lying, it'll add another six months to your sentence."

"Is that all?"

The lawman looked at him. "I've worn a tin star long enough, I can feel it in my bones when someone is trouble. And you're as much trouble as they come."

"Why, you sweet-talking devil, you."

Mako let that pass and said, "Which is why I'm taking extra precautions. Those cuffs stay on, so get used to them. And I'll make it plain to my deputies that if you give them any guff, I won't mind a bit if they kick your teeth down your throat."

"So much for the sweet talk."

"I don't like your kind," Marshal Mako said coldly. "Not even a little bit."

"What kind is that? Scouts?"

"It's not what you do. It's you. You're one of those who thinks he can do as he damn well pleases, and the rest of the world be damned."

"Last I heard," Fargo said, "this is a free country."

"A country with laws. Laws that you reckon aren't good enough for you to follow."

"When the law says a man can't spit without being arrested," Fargo said, "that's a pretty damn dumb law."

"You just made my point. It's not what a law says. It's the fact that it's a law. I'm paid to make sure folks abide by them, whether they want to abide by them or not."

"That mayor and you make a good pair," Fargo said. "It's too bad you don't have your own country to run."

"This town will do," Mako said. "And before I forget, a word to the wise. If you try to escape, we'll shoot you dead. Army or no army."

"Escape is the furthest thing from my mind."

"Like hell."

On that note Fargo was shoved back into his cell and the door clanged shut once again.

Over the next couple of days he paid close attention to their routine.

Mako was only there during the day. At night the deputies worked shifts. Brock had the first, Gergan the second, Clyde the last. Each morning the prisoners were roused and herded into the prison wagon for another day's work.

Twice a day they brought Fargo food. They always slid the plate through a wide slot in the bars rather than open the door.

All in all, it was a well-run jail.

But there was a weak spot.

The third night, Gergan propped his boots on the desk, folded his arms and pulled his hat low, and dozed off.

Hiking his pant leg, Fargo palmed the Arkansas toothpick. They had made light of his buckskins, but buckskins had one thing city-bought clothes didn't: whangs. His were six inches long on his shirt. He cut ten of them off, replaced the knife in his boot, and tied the whangs together, end to end.

Moving to the bars, he crouched. He fashioned a loop and positioned it on the floor directly under the food slot. Drawing the end inside, he tied it to the bottom of a bar.

Returning to the bunk, he lay with his back to the room.

Deputy Clyde showed up to relieve Gergan. No sooner was Gergan out the door than Clyde sat down at the desk and propped his boots as Gergan had done.

Fargo got up and went close to the bars. But not too close. "Deputy," he called out.

Clyde raised his head. "What do *you* want?" he asked suspiciously.

"Some water," Fargo said. "My throat's dry."

"Tough."

"One glass," Fargo said, "and you can take your usual nap."

"I'll take it anyway. And you can wait until breakfast."

"Would you do it for a dollar?"

"Nice try," Clyde said, "but the marshal took your poke."

"I had a loose dollar in my pocket," Fargo said.

Clyde showed interest. Deputies didn't make a lot of money. "I give you the glass, you shut the hell up and let me sleep?"

"That's the deal."

Reluctantly Clyde stood and went to the water pitcher. He filled a glass and brought it over, his other hand on his six-gun. "No tricks."

"All I want is a drink," Fargo said. And to get the hell out of that cage.

"Not that there's much you can do," Clyde said.

Fargo held his cuffed wrists out. "Isn't that the truth?"

Deputy Clyde stopped in front of the slot. In the dim light from the single lamp, he didn't spot the loop on the floor even though his left foot was partly in it. "Here," he said, and passed the glass through.

"I'm obliged," Fargo said as he stepped up and took it in both hands. He raised it to his mouth but paused when Clyde turned. "Shouldn't you take the glass with you?"

"What for?"

"I might break it and try to cut one of you with the broken glass."

"That would be a damn fool stunt," Deputy Clyde said, but he turned back. "Hurry up and drink and give it to me."

His left foot was in the middle of the loop.

Fargo drank half the glass in two gulps and held it to the slot.

"That's all you wanted?" Clyde reached to take it from

him. "And where's that dollar you promised? You'd better not have been lying."

"Me lie?" Fargo said, and streaked his hands to the whang cord. Grabbing it, he gave a powerful jerk; the loop slid up around Clyde's ankle and fastened tight.

"What the hell?" Clyde blurted.

Fargo wrenched, slamming Clyde's leg against the bars. Swearing, Clyde let go of the glass and clawed for his six-shooter. His face was near the bars.

Quick as thought, Fargo thrust his hand through the slot. As hard as he could, he drove his rigid fingers into Clyde's neck. Once, twice, and again.

Clyde cried out. His eyelids fluttered. He tried to pull his leg away and couldn't. He twisted, which put his holster close to the slot.

A flick of Fargo's fingers, and the deputy's Remington was his. Cocking it, he growled, "Try to run and I'll splatter your guts."

Clyde groped his empty holster. Sagging against the cell, he groaned.

Fargo thrust the revolver's barrel into his. "Did you hear me?"

"Run?" Clyde gasped, a hand to his neck. "I can't hardly stand."

Fargo glanced past him at a peg on the wall. On it hung a large brass ring with the keys. "You're going to fetch the key and let me out."

Sucking in deep breaths, Clyde said, "You'll get ten years for this."

"You won't live ten minutes if you don't do as I tell you."

"Go easy on that trigger. I have no hankering to die."

Fargo told him to free his leg from the loop.

Still wobbly, Clyde had to try several times and nearly fell, but he managed to slide it off. "Clever," he said. "I never would've thought of this."

"Get the keys," Fargo commanded. "Try to run—"

"I know, I know," Clyde said. He staggered to the peg and brought the ring over. The first key he inserted didn't work.

"Quit stalling."

"I can't hardly think," Clyde complained. "It's a wonder you didn't kill me."

"The night's not over yet."

Clyde looked at him in new fear. "Hold on, now. I'm doing what you want, ain't I?"

"Get the goddamn door open."

Working faster, Clyde succeeded. "There." He pulled the door open, and groaned. "I don't feel so good."

"Inside," Fargo said. Not content to wait, he took hold of the scruff of Clyde's neck and pushed him.

Clyde stumbled and fell to one knee. Easing onto the bunk, he cradled his head and said through his fingers, "There's nowhere you can run that the marshal won't find you. He'll have circulars made and send them all over Texas."

"Who said anything about running?" Fargo closed the cell door and went to the front window. Moving the shade, he peered out.

The street was as empty as a cemetery.

Fargo made sure the front door was bolted, then moved toward the back.

"Hold on," Deputy Clyde said. "What in God's name are you fixing to do?"

"Raise hell," Fargo said.

11

It was easy to tell which key to use on the padlock on the barracks door; it was bigger than all the rest. Fargo dropped the padlock to the dirt and picked up the lamp he had set down while he opened it.

Inside was dark as pitch. As the light spread, it revealed the sleeping forms of the prisoners. It was a hot night and many hadn't bothered pulling their single blanket up. They were a haggard bunch. The hard labor and bad food had taken a toll.

Fargo stepped to a lantern on a peg and set to lighting it.

Some of the men stirred. They mumbled, blinked, shifted. Chains rattled and clanked.

One man squinted and raised a hand in front of his eyes to protect them from the glare. "What's goin' on?" he croaked.

Another sat up and looked about in confusion. "It can't be morning yet."

Fargo raised both the lamp and the lantern over his head. The light reached clear to the partition that separated the men from the women. "Wake up. All of you. You're getting out of here."

More of them woke, some mumbling and grumbling.

"Somethin' is goin' on!" the first man hollered. "They're up to somethin' new."

Fargo waited for them to rouse. Dawn wasn't for three hours or so, more than enough time for what he had in mind. "Keep it down," he cautioned. "You don't want to make a ruckus that will bring the marshal."

A grizzled apparition bent toward him. "Aren't you one of his deputies?"

"I sure as hell am not," Fargo declared. "I'm here to free you."

Stunned expressions spread like wildfire.

"What did you say?" the grizzled man asked. "I must not have heard right."

"I'm here to free you," Fargo repeated.

All of them were up and staring at him in surprise, disbelief, and hope.

"How's that again?" a prisoner farther back said. "Did you say free us?"

"Is this some sort of trick?" another asked.

Fargo moved down the aisle between the bunks until he was midway. "Listen close. I'm not with the marshal. I was in jail. I broke out. Now I aim to break all of you out."

"You're serious?" a scarecrow bleated.

"God in heaven!" another exclaimed.

"I have the keys," Fargo said, and gave the ring a shake. "I'll free a couple of you and they can free the rest and we'll get the hell out of here."

"You *are* serious?" the scarecrow said, and his eyes filled with tears.

"If Mako catches us, him and his deputies will shoot us down like dogs," another man mentioned fearfully.

"They're nowhere around," Fargo assured them. "Now, are you with me or not?"

Their initial shock was fading. A number of them swapped glances and nodded and then one man let out with, "Hell yes, we're with you." Another yipped for joy.

"Quiet down, damn it!" Fargo cut their elation short. "Do you want to wake half the town?"

Silence fell, and many looked anxiously at the front door.

"That's better," Fargo said. He set down the lamp and moved to the partition. "Ladies first. Then I'll be back to free you. Be ready."

All three of the females were up: Carmody Wells, the young one with freckles, and the woman who had to be in her fifties.

"You heard?" Fargo said as he stepped to Carmody's bunk. She stared as if she couldn't believe her eyes.

"You came for me."

"And these others."

"You came for me," she said again. "Why? Most men wouldn't have bothered."

"Let's just say," Fargo remarked as he bent to the metal band around her ankle, "I don't much care for sons of bitches who beat on women."

"You're really here to free us?" the freckled one said. She wasn't much past twenty, with brunette hair clipped short below her ears. It lent her a pixie quality enhanced by her big green eyes.

"This is Alice Thorn," Carmody introduced her. "The other lady is Sarabeth."

Fargo tried a key, but it didn't work.

The older woman had her hands to her throat. "I don't know about this. I truly don't."

"Sara?" Carmody said.

"I only have a few months left on my sentence," Sarabeth said. "If we escape and they catch us—" She shuddered.

"They won't catch you," Fargo said as he tried a second key.

"You don't know that," Sarabeth said. "The marshal will get up a posse."

The clamp opened, revealing discolored flesh and red lines where the band had chafed and bitten into Carmody's flesh.

"Thank you," Carmody said softly.

Working quickly, Fargo freed the other two. Alice Thorn jumped up and rubbed her ankle, but Sarabeth slid back on her bed and shook her head.

"No, sir. I'm not going. I won't have time added. I couldn't take it."

"Sara," Carmody said. "Please."

"No, I say."

Fargo had no time for this. "Talk her into it if you can while I free the men." Hurrying out, he found them eagerly perched on the ends of their bunks. Some held their chains and shook them in impatience.

"Hurry up, mister."

"We want the hell out of here."

"Do we ever!"

The same key that had freed the women worked for the men. Fargo let loose two and gave them the ring. "Do the others."

"Lickety-split," one replied.

Fargo went to the front door and stepped outside. He listened but heard only the sigh of the wind and the mew of a cat. Not a single light glowed anywhere. The good people of Fairplay were tucked in their beds. He hoped to hell they stayed there.

A sound drew him to the jail. He peered in and discovered that Deputy Clyde had removed his belt and was trying to jimmy the cell door lock with the prong. Quietly slipping in, Fargo was almost to the cell before Clyde noticed him and sprang back.

"I wasn't doing anything!" Clyde yelped, and tried to hide the belt behind his leg.

Fargo held out his hand. "Hand it over."

"Hand what over?" Clyde asked innocently.

Placing his hand on the Remington, Fargo asked, "How stupid are you?"

"Damn it," Clyde said. But he slid the buckle between the bars. "It wasn't working anyhow."

Fargo dropped the belt on the desk. He checked at the front window; the street was still deserted. Satisfied, he went out the back again, saying, "Make any noise and you'll regret it."

"Mister," Deputy Clyde replied, "the only one who will regret this is you."

A few prisoners were still shackled, but they wouldn't be for long. The rest of the men had gathered near the door.

Carmody and Alice were there, too, but not Sarabeth.

"The coast is still clear," Fargo informed them. "In twenty minutes we'll be on our way out of town."

"I sure hope so," one said. "I've had my fill of this hell-hole."

"What's your handle?"

"Franklyn Immelt. Just call me Frank."

"Have them line up," Fargo directed. "When I give the word, we're heading for the stable. No talking. No yelling. Savvy?"

Frank bobbed his head. "We'll be as quiet as mice."

The last man of them was being freed.

Fargo turned in the doorway, and a warm hand touched his neck.

"I want to thank you again," Carmody Wells said softly.

"Later would be better."

"There might not be a chance," Carmody said. "I want you to know that whatever else happens, I'm sticking with you."

Fargo had them extinguish the lamp and the lantern. He told them that if they couldn't see that well, to hold the hand of the person in front. "Whatever you do, don't fall behind."

"Don't worry about that," Frank said.

"We want out of here more than you can imagine," another prisoner declared.

Carmody put her lips near to Fargo's ear. "Did you say something about holding hands?" she said, and clasped his.

Fargo led the way. They went around the jail to a side street and along it toward the stable. They had several blocks to cover. He stuck to the darkest patches and stopped at the slightest sounds.

They only had one block to go when the clomp of hooves caused Fargo freeze in place.

A rider was coming up the next street over.

Hunkering, Fargo pulled Carmody down beside him. The rest promptly dropped low, too.

"Who can it be?" Alice whispered.

"Quiet," Fargo warned.

The thuds grew louder.

Fargo glimpsed a big man on a big horse heading in the direction of the jail. His gut tightened. The rider's size worried him. He'd only seen one person in Fairplay that big: Deputy Brock. Fargo had no idea what Brock was doing up and about so early. But if he was right, all hell would soon break loose.

Up and moving before the clomps faded, Fargo went twice as fast. He would run except the prisoners weren't in the best of shape.

The stable was shut for the night, the wide double doors barred.

Fargo told the others to stay put while he slipped around to the back. A couple of horses were in the corral and neither whinnied or stamped. He climbed over the rails and tried the rear door. It wasn't bolted.

Once inside, Fargo hesitated. Should he get his Colt from his saddlebags or let the others in?

He ran to the front, raised the heavy bar, and set it to one side.

No sooner had he pulled on one of the wide doors than a shot shattered the night.

12

The prisoners were frozen in alarm, many with their heads cocked in the direction the shot came from: the marshal's office.

"What can it mean?" Frank gave voice to their fear.

There was another shot and then shouts. Deputy Brock began bellowing, "They've escaped! The prisoners have escaped!"

"He'll rouse the whole town!" a prisoner exclaimed.

"We have to hide!" another cried, and bolted into the darkness.

"Come back!" Fargo snapped, but the harm had been done. Their fear blossomed into panic. Seven or eight ran after the first, and a moment later almost all the rest scattered. He was left standing there with Carmody, Alice, and Frank.

"The jackasses," the latter declared. "They can't get away on foot."

"Inside," Fargo urged, and after they quickly obeyed, he replaced the bar on the doors. "Pick a horse," he said. "Any horse."

No one argued that horse stealing was wrong or that it would add to their time behind bars if they were caught.

For Fargo's part, he raced to the Ovaro's stall. First he opened his saddlebag and hurriedly strapped on his Colt. Then he threw on his saddle blanket and saddle.

Somewhere in the distance more yells were raised. Another shot cracked and someone screamed.

Acutely conscious that each passing second increased their danger, Fargo got a bridle on and brought the stallion out.

The others were already on mounts. Only Carmody had bothered with a saddle.

"As soon as the door is open," Fargo instructed, "we break to the right and ride like hell. Once we're out of town, we'll head west."

"If we make it out," Carmody said.

"Don't talk like that," Alice Thorn said. "I'm never letting them get their hands on me again."

Bedlam had been unleashed. Fairplay was in the grip of a spreading cacophony of cries and a riot of hammering feet.

Raising the heavy bar once more, Fargo moved it out of the way and dropped it. Not wasting a moment, he forked leather, kicked the door open, and with twin jabs of his spurs he was out into the night. The others were right behind him. He wheeled the Ovaro and was almost to an intersection when a man in a nightshirt huffed from a house waving a shotgun.

"Hold on there, you people! Stop or I'll by God shoot!"

The man made the mistake of running out in front of them.

Another jab of Fargo's spurs and the Ovaro slammed into him like a four-legged battering ram. Squawking, the man went flying one way and his shotgun another.

Fargo didn't look back to see how badly the man was hurt. He didn't give a damn.

In the next street half a dozen townsfolk were milling in confusion. Several pointed and a woman yelled and a six-gun flared.

Fargo answered in kind. He shot high, at the shoulder instead of the chest, and saw the man fold. His conscience pricked him for shooting someone who was only trying to stop a jailbreak.

He reminded himself that the good people of Fairplay didn't mind being lorded over by their high-handed mayor and vicious marshal, and deserved whatever happened to them.

The other townsfolk fled.

At the next junction Fargo reined left. It was six blocks yet to the outskirts. Once they were in the open, they stood a good chance of leaving pursuit far behind.

A rider galloped out of an alley, cutting them off. It was Deputy Gergan, a revolver in his hand. Gergan didn't order them to stop. He pointed his six-gun and snapped off a shot.

Fargo heard Frank cry out. Fargo fired, and Gergan was jolted half out of his saddle but clung on and raised his revolver to shoot again. Fargo sent a second slug into him. Then they were past and the deputy was upside down, hanging by a boot hooked in a stirrup.

"You killed him!" Carmody cried.

What the hell did she expect? Fargo wondered. It was root hog or die, and he was fond of breathing. He flew the last five blocks. No one tried to stop them. No lead was slung.

Once the last building was behind them, he slowed so the others could catch up. Carmody and Alice were fine, but Frank was doubled over and clinging to his saddle horn.

"How bad?" Fargo asked.

"Keep going. I can make it."

Fargo took him at his word and rode on, the women on either side. They were as grim as death, aware of the stakes. Neither said a word.

More shots boomed back in town. More shouts added to the discord.

Fargo was glad to be out of there. He wouldn't put it past Stoddard and Mako to put out wanted circulars on them, and he'd deal with that later. Right now the important thing was to put as much distance as they could behind them.

They covered half a mile. A mile.

Pale starlight bathed the road and the high grass, lending the illusion of peace and serenity.

At a holler from Carmody, Fargo glanced over his shoulder and drew rein.

Frank had fallen behind. He was swaying and had one hand splayed to his chest. Almost too late, he reined up to keep from colliding with them.

"You let us think it wasn't that bad," Fargo said.

Frank showed his teeth in a lighthearted grin. "I did, didn't I? I lied." He laughed, or tried to, and froth spilled from his lips.

"Hell," Fargo said. Dismounting, he reached up. "Lean on me," he directed, and carefully eased the thin man down. "Can you stand?"

"No," Frank said, and started to collapse. A stain darkened much of his shirt.

"Easy." Fargo lowered him onto his back.

Carmody sank to her knees and clasped Frank's hand in both of hers. "No," she said softly. "No, no, no. You treated me the nicest of just about anybody."

"You're a good gal," Frank said, wheezing. "They did you wrong like they did the rest of us. You should keep going before they catch up."

Fargo stared back along the road. "No one is after us yet."

"I won't leave you like this," Carmody said to Frank "You've been a friend."

Frank coughed, and more froth dribbled from his mouth. "I won't have them catch you on account of me. Get on your nag and light a shuck."

"Not on your life."

"Not on yours, either," Frank said. "Listen to me, girl, before it's too late."

74

It already was. Fargo spied four-legged stick figures far off. "I spoke too soon," he said. "Here they come."

"Go," Frank said, and tried to push Carmody, but he was too weak.

"I'm not leaving and that's final."

Frank looked up at Fargo. "Please, mister. Do what has to be done. They get their paws on her, it'll be twice as bad as before."

Fargo put his hand on Carmody's arm. "He's right. We have to go."

"No."

"They'll be here in a couple of minutes."

"I don't care. He's my friend, damn it."

Frank coughed and limply held out his arm to Fargo. "Please," he pleaded.

"Hell," Fargo said. Suddenly looping his arm around Carmody, he bodily lifted her, took a step, and swung her up and over her animal. In reflex, she spread her legs and grabbed the mane to keep from falling.

"No, I told you!"

"Go," Frank said.

Fargo pointed at the riders. There were four of them, coming hard, raising a cloud a dust. "We don't have time for this."

Carmody uttered a sob and tried to climb down, but Fargo wouldn't let her.

"Stay up there, damn you."

"I won't leave him!"

Alice Thorn stepped over to Frank and raised her right leg. Before they could guess her intent, she stomped her foot down on Frank's throat. Frank gurgled and arched his back.

"No!" Carmody cried.

"What the hell?" Fargo said, and spun, but he couldn't reach Alice before she brought her foot down a second time. The *crunch* was as clear as anything.

Frank bucked, spewed blood, and was gone.

"Now we can go," Alice Thorn said.

"Alice, damn you!" Carmody cried. Again she tried to dismount.

Fargo almost lost his hold on her, he was so shocked. Shoving her upright, he pointed at the body. "He's gone. There's nothing you can do."

Carmody quaked and said with tears streaming down her cheeks, "Alice, how could you?"

The freckle-faced woman didn't answer. As calmly as if she were going on a Sunday ride, she climbed back on her bay and raised the reins. "I'm ready when you are."

Stepping into the stirrups, Fargo checked on their pursuers. He reckoned they were a quarter mile off yet. "Fan the breeze," he said, and when both women broke into a gallop, he did likewise.

For long minutes they raced. Here and there a low hill reared. They had gone another two miles or so when Fargo called another halt.

"Why are we stopping?" Alice demanded. "I can ride all night if I have to."

"Your horse can't," Fargo said, nodding at her winded animal. "We'll give them a breather." Not that the Ovaro needed one. The stallion possessed exceptional stamina.

Alice gazed back. "I don't see them after us anymore."

"They stopped at the body," Fargo guessed. "It won't delay them long." He paused. "Answer me something."

"If I can."

"Why?"

"That's easy," Alice said. "He wasn't long for this world anyway. And he wanted us to go. You heard him."

"Still," Fargo said.

Carmody was in a pit of misery. "He was my friend. I'll never forgive you, Alice. Not ever."

"We're alive," Alice said. "We wouldn't be if we'd stuck with him."

"That's awful cold," Carmody criticized. "You killed him to save your hide."

"*Our* hides," Alice corrected her. "And I'd do it again."

Fargo would never have guessed she had it in her. She seemed so innocent, so . . . sweet. "We need to ride, ladies."

"You'll get no argument from me," Alice said. To Carmody she said, "Your friend is dead. Get over it." And she smacked her legs against her mount.

Caromody followed.

Fargo stayed at her side. They held to a trot for half a mile or more, until Fargo called out to Alice that she was pushing too hard.

"I don't care," she hollered back. "It's not my horse."

"You'll care if you ride it into the ground and Mako gets his hands on you."

"All right, all right," Alice said, slowing.

"She's something, that one," Carmody remarked.

"How long did she have left on her sentence?" Fargo wondered.

"Fifteen years."

"That long?" Fargo said, and joked, "What did she do? Kill someone?"

"Didn't I tell you?" Carmody said. "Little Alice murdered two men. And she admits it, too."

13

It bothered him.

Fargo had taken it for granted that most of the people who ended up in Fairplay's "barracks" didn't deserve to be there. He figured that Stoddard and Mako had done to them as they did to him.

Now he wasn't so sure.

They couldn't trump up a pair of murders.

He realized he might have freed someone who should rightfully be behind bars.

And it bothered him.

They rode until noon. That there was no pursuit surprised him.

Their horses needed rest. So did they. The country was more wooded, and he called a halt in a grove of trees that bordered the road. With his back to an oak and the Henry across his lap, he watched the way they had come.

Carmody curled on her side and closed her eyes to nap.

As for freckled Alice Thorn, she hunkered, facing them, and idly plucked blades of grass.

"You don't want to sleep?" Fargo said.

She shook her head.

"It's been a rough night."

"All we did was ride."

"You killed a man," Fargo reminded her.

"I put him out of his misery," Alice said. "Same as I'd do for any critter."

"Is that what you did to the two people I hear you murdered?"

"No," Alice said, continuing to pluck grass. "They deserved it."

"Mind if I ask how?"

"They tried to have their way with me."

"Did you know them?"

Showing no emotion whatsoever, Alice said, "I'm from east Texas. I was on my way to San Antonio by stage. I have kin there. An aunt. The vermin I killed were on the stage, too. Louts, the pair of them. Kept ogling me. Kept making remarks. I told them to shut their mouths, but they wouldn't listen. One said as how they weren't afraid of a sweet little thing like me." She uttered an icy laugh.

Fargo waited.

"Anyhow, we stopped in Fairplay," Alice resumed. "It was evening. I got out to stretch my legs, and the louts went to a saloon. The stage was supposed to head out again in an hour. I was sitting out behind the stage office, minding my own business, when they jumped me. Tried to rip off my britches so they could have a poke."

"And?" Fargo prompted.

"What do you think? I had a knife in my boot. I slit the one's throat."

Again he had to prompt her. "The other one?"

"I stuck the blade in his balls. He flopped and shrieked until I cut off his pecker and stuffed it down his throat to shut him up."

"Son of a bitch."

"They both were. I didn't know it but the owner of the stage line saw me out the window and told the marshal. Next thing, Mako arrested me and took me before that no-account judge. I told them how it was self-defense, but that Stoddard fella said I was a menace to the community and sentenced me to eighteen years."

Fargo remembered what Carmody had told him. "You've been a prisoner for three years?"

Alice nodded grimly. "Years I can never get back."

"You're free now," Fargo said.

"Thanks to you, and I'm obliged. But being free ain't enough."

"How do you mean?"

She didn't reply, and Fargo didn't press it. He believed her account.

Anywhere else but Fairplay, she'd have been acquitted.

Taking off his hat, Fargo leaned back. Save for the chirping of some sparrows, the woods were quiet. The serenity and the heat got to him. He became drowsy. Twice he closed his eyes and snapped them open again. The third time, he dozed off.

He'd been up all night and it caught up to him. He slept so soundly that when a jay squawked, he sat up, startled, and looked around in alarm.

The first thing he noticed was that, judging by the sun, he'd slept a couple of hours. The second thing was that his Henry wasn't in his lap. The third thing was that Alice wasn't hunkered across from him.

Fargo glanced around and discovered something else. Alice's bay was missing, too. "What the hell?" he blurted. Jamming his hat on, he pushed to his feet. "Alice?" he called out.

Carmody stirred and rose on an elbow. Yawning, she said, "What's the ruckus about?"

"Your friend left and took my rifle with her."

"That sounds like something Alice would do," Carmody said, sitting up. "She's a tough one, that girl."

"We're going after her," Fargo said, and turned toward their horses.

"What for?"

"Didn't you hear me? She stole my rifle."

"And she'll likely have it with her when we catch up," Carmody said. "We rush off in this heat, we'll only have to stop again in a couple of hours. Why not rest until it cools down?"

All Fargo could think of was his rifle. "I don't want to lose her."

"You won't," Carmody said. "There's only the one road." She patted the ground. "Have a seat. We can pass the time together."

Her hooded eyes, and the playful manner in which she puckered her lips, gave him pause.

"Well?" Carmody teased. "Are you just going to stand there?"

Fargo checked to the east. There wasn't a rider in sight. Not even a tendril of dust. He looked at Carmody, at her loose hair and her full lips, at the swell of her shirt and the curve of her thighs. "You pick a damn strange time."

"Do you know how long it's been? I'm not a nun or a schoolmarm."

Fargo realized how little he knew about her. "What were you before Stoddard got hold of you?"

"I was a dove," Carmody said. "I worked in saloons."

"The hell you say."

"I came to Fairplay with my best friend, Jugs. We were about broke, so we hired on at the Tumbleweed. Wasn't long before a clerk at the general store took a shine to me and wanted a tumble for money." Carmody shook her head sadly. "I took him up on it and the marshal found out and arrested me."

"How did he find out?"

"That damned clerk. He bragged to his friends and one of them went to Mako. It seems if you turn somebody in, you get paid."

"That sounds like Stoddard's doing."

"Let's forget about that bastard for a while." Brazenly

reaching up, Carmody cupped him. "Come on. You know you want to."

"Damn it," Fargo said, but he didn't move.

Carmody grinned and squeezed, and rubbed, and suddenly he was as hard as iron. "Oh my. Don't try to tell me you don't want to."

Fargo couldn't answer for the lump in his throat. To hell with it, he thought, and sank to his knees.

"I must not look very pretty at the moment," Carmody said, while with her other hand she plucked at her shirt. "Sorry about these clothes. They make the men wear stripes, but us women get store-bought duds."

Fargo checked the road to town again. Nothing. A quick one wouldn't hurt, he reckoned, and cupped both her breasts.

Carmody stiffened and gasped and threw back her head. "Oh God. It's been so long."

Fargo felt a shiver run through her. "You weren't joshing about wanting it."

"You have no idea," Carmody said.

The next instant her lips were fastened to his. She didn't so much kiss him as try to suck his mouth into hers.

Reaching behind her, Fargo cupped her bottom. In response she thrust her body at his and ground her nether mound against his hardness.

Fargo went to unbutton her shirt, but again she took the initiative and near frantically unfastened his gun belt so she could tug his buckskin shirt out and slide her hands underneath.

"Goodness," she exclaimed. "You're all muscles."

"The biggest is between my legs."

"So I noticed." Carmody grinned and renewed her stroking.

Covering her mouth with his, Fargo got her shirt open. Her breasts were warm and firm. When he pinched a nipple, she sank her teeth into his shoulder.

Fargo winced, and pinched her, hard. It set her hips to moving in circles and she panted like a bellows.

"God in heaven, how I want you," Carmody husked into his ear.

Easing her down, Fargo stretched out and went to peel her pants off, but once again she couldn't wait. She pushed his hand away and did it herself.

The lust in her eyes, her full, pouty lips, the peaks of her tits, and those smooth, creamy legs below her thatch set his blood to burning.

His hands were everywhere, as were hers. She scratched. She bit. She incited him with pain as much as pleasure.

She liked it rough, and he obliged.

There came the moment when he was poised between her legs, his hands on her hips. She looked into his eyes and said throatily, "Do it."

Fargo rammed up and in.

She cried out, clamped her legs around him, and rode him as if he were a bronc and she were his saddle.

They went at it furious and fast until their mutual explosion brought them half up off the ground.

"Oh!" Carmody gushed. "Oh! Oh! Oh!"

All Fargo did was growl.

Afterward, he lay on top of her, both of them wet with sweat, her breasts cushioning his chest, her lips pressed to his throat.

"Thank you," she said softly. "I needed that."

Fargo was about to say that he did, too, when their idyllic moment was brought to an end by the boom of a gunshot.

14

The shot came from off to the east, which puzzled Fargo. He wondered if it was the posse. Maybe signaling. But to whom? Rising, he began to put himself back together.

"Who could that be?" Carmody asked, imitating him.

"Just about anyone."

They climbed on their mounts and moved to the road. In both directions it was empty.

"I don't see anyone," Carmody said. "Let's keep going. The last thing I want is for Marshal Mako to get his hands on me again."

Fargo recollected the incident he'd witnessed through the window. "How did he treat you?"

"Most of the time he was decent enough. But now and then I'd catch him looking at me as if . . ." Carmody stopped.

"As if what?"

"I don't rightly know." She shrugged. "As if he had something in mind I'd rather not think about."

"You don't mean—?"

"I told you. I don't know. Probably not. One time a male prisoner tried to grope me, and Mako broke both his hands."

"Tough hombre," Fargo said.

"Dangerous hombre," Carmody amended. "You can see it in his eyes. He's vicious when he wants to be. But he has respect for the law."

"Horatio Stoddard's law."

"I mentioned that to Mako once. I said it's not right to say who can and can't make love, and how much people can gamble, and things like that."

"What did he say?"

"He agreed, if you can believe it. He stood there and flat out said some of the town's laws are stupid. But it's his job to enforce them anyway."

"He's not out to fleece folks?"

"Not him. The mayor, yes. Stoddard imposes fines that go into his bank account and gets all that free labor to work at his ranch."

She would have gone on, but just then hooves drummed. They both started and straightened.

Out of the east flew a horse. Riderless, it came at a gallop and would have swept on by if Fargo hadn't cut it off and grabbed its trailing reins to bring it to a halt.

The horse tossed its mane and stamped but didn't attempt to break away.

Carmody came up and was the first to notice. "Say, what's that all over the saddle?"

Fargo bent. It was blood. A lot of it. Larger patches near the saddle horn with smaller drops behind and lower down. "Whoever was on this was gut-shot."

"How can you tell?"

"The pattern," Fargo said. "I've seen it before." He'd been in plenty of skirmishes with hostiles and seen a lot of troopers wounded by lead, arrows, and lances. Turning in the saddle, he peered east. "I'm going back."

"What?" Carmody's eyes widened. "We're in the clear. We should push on."

"I want to know who was shot."

"Who cares, damn it?" Carmody said. "Besides, what about your precious rifle? We have to go after Alice, remember, and she went west."

"Did she?" Fargo said. "I wonder." He scanned the dirt

road to the west. Puzzled, he dismounted and searched on foot. "I'll be damned."

"What now?"

"There aren't any fresh tracks. She didn't go west, after all."

"You must be mistaken."

"Not about tracks." If there was one thing Fargo did better than just about anyone, it was read sign. It was why the army considered him one of the best scouts alive. He climbed back on the Ovaro, snagged the other animal's reins, and wheeled to the east.

"This is dumb," Carmody said. "We're asking for trouble."

"You don't have to come."

"Damn you," she said, and did.

Fargo scoured for sign, becoming more puzzled the farther they went. After half a mile, he remarked, "She didn't come this way, either."

"What are you saying? Alice cut across country to the north or the south? She'd have to be dumber than you. We're in the middle of Comanche territory, in case you've forgotten."

The next moment Fargo spotted a body, belly down in the middle of the road. He tapped his spurs and was out of the saddle before the stallion stopped moving.

A pool of scarlet formed a body-sized halo. It was more—much more—than a human being could lose and go on breathing.

Fargo rolled it over.

The man was in his twenties and wore store-bought clothes. A derby lay nearby, upside down. The slug had entered above his groin and left an exit wound close to his spine.

To Fargo's surprise, the man's eyelids fluttered and opened.

"God," he said.

"Who did this?" Fargo asked.

The man seemed to struggle to focus. "One of you."

"Like hell," Carmody said. "Neither of us put lead in you, mister."

"The other gal," the man barely got out. "The one with brown hair and freckles." He groaned and weakly placed a hand over his belly. "God, I hurt."

"Brown hair and freckles?" Carmody repeated, incredulous. "Alice Thorn?"

"She shot me with no warning," the townsman said. "From off in the grass."

Fargo stepped to the edge of the road and discovered a flattened trail where a horse had emerged. He realized that Alice must have been paralleling the road the whole time. Which was why he didn't find her tracks. It was clever. Very clever.

"I never saw her," the townsman gasped. "I think she made her horse lie down and picked me off when I got close."

Fargo came back over. "You're with the posse?"

The man managed to nod. "They sent me on ahead. My horse was faster than theirs. I was to find you and get word back to them." He closed his eyes and groaned louder. "God, now I'm cold. I'm not long for this world, am I?"

Carmody glanced at Fargo, and Fargo shook his head.

"I'm sorry," she said to the townsman. "I never wanted anyone hurt."

"Then you're not like that other one," the man said. "She stood over me and smiled and told me I got what I deserved."

Carmody said, "You're not our enemy. The mayor is. Him and his tin-star flunkies."

"Your friend aims to kill them, too. Her and that shiny rifle of hers."

Fargo frowned.

"How do you know?" Carmody asked, but the man didn't seem to hear. Gently shaking his arm, she asked it again.

His eyes opened partway. Wearily, he said, "She told me, is how. She stood right there and said she intends to kill Mayor Stoddard and the marshal and everyone else who had a hand in putting her behind bars. She even aims to kill the mayor's daughter."

"Hell," Fargo said.

The townsman shivered. "I asked her to put me out of my misery, but she refused. She said it was right I suffer. Me and all the rest she's after."

"You think you know someone," Carmody said, more to herself than to either of them.

"I don't want to die. I honest to God do not—" The townsman gazed at the sky, said simply, "Oh!" and breathed his last.

"He never told us his name," Carmody said. "Do we bury him?"

Fargo had a more important matter to tend to. "I'm heading for town."

Rising, Carmody clasped his arm. "What in hell for?"

"You heard him," Fargo said. "She killed him with my Henry."

"So?"

"So it's *my* Henry."

"What difference does that make? You can always buy another. Why risk your life going back there when you don't have to?"

Fargo climbed on the Ovaro. It would be pointless to try and overtake Alice. She had too much of a lead. He held to a walk and chafed at having to do so.

Carmody quickly caught up. "You didn't answer me."

"What do you know about her?"

"Alice? She didn't talk a lot. Not about herself, anyhow. She was raised on a farm, as I recall."

"That's all?"

"She hunted a lot when she was a little girl. Meat for the

table, mostly. Rabbits and squirrels and such. Once she shot a black bear."

"So she's damn good with a gun."

"And she can ride as good as a man. She bragged as much."

"It gets better and better," Fargo said.

"You wouldn't know it to look at her," Carmody said, "but she's as tough as they come."

"Is she as good as her word?"

"I never knew her to tell a lie, if that's what you mean."

"No," Fargo said. "Will she carry out her threat to kill Stoddard and whoever else she has in mind?"

"I suppose. Again, what difference does it make? I won't lose any sleep over it and neither should you."

No, Fargo wouldn't, but he continued to the east.

"Why are you doing this?" Carmody asked. "If they get hold of you, they'll slap a leg iron on and you'll be digging ditches and planting crops from now until doomsday."

Fargo didn't answer.

"Damn it," Carmody snapped. "I don't understand, and I'd like to."

"I already told you."

"Because she has your stupid rifle?"

Fargo grunted.

"What kind of reason is that? I refuse—you hear me? I refuse to go back there and be chained like some animal all over again."

"No one is forcing you."

"Please don't."

"Head west if you want. In six or seven days you'll reach a settlement called Travis."

"Go all that way by my lonesome? With Comanches and God knows what else out there?" Carmody glared. "I hate this. I pray you know what in hell you're doing."

Fargo didn't say anything, but so did he.

15

Half a mile farther they heard more shots. Four blasts in quick cadence—*bam, bam, bam, bam*—which hinted to Fargo that the shooter was sure of his target.

They spied the bodies from a hundred yards out, four sprawled figures at the side of the road.

Fargo drew his Colt and they cautiously advanced. He didn't need to examine the fallen to be sure they were dead. All four had been shot in the head.

Dismounting, he roved about, reconstructing the sign. Two horses were off in the grass, grazing. The other two had run off.

Carmody stayed on her mount, her features a mirror of disbelief. "Alice did this?"

"Appears so," Fargo said.

"Sweet, quiet, little Alice?"

"It's the posse that man we found earlier was with. He went on ahead while they stopped to rest and waited for him to report back, remember?"

"I don't see the marshal."

"Mako wasn't with it." Fargo rolled one of the bodies over. "This one was."

"Deputy Clyde!" Carmody exclaimed.

The weasel had been hit smack between the eyes. In death he was even uglier than in life.

Fargo noticed something else. "See that watch lying

there? And that folding knife? She went through their pockets and pokes."

"She robbed them?"

Fargo came to the last man. A revolver lay next to him, but he wasn't wearing a gun belt. The revolver was the same caliber as Fargo's Henry. "She got hold of more ammunition."

"And rode on to town?" Carmody gazed eastward. "Dear God. What does she think she can do?"

"Haven't you been paying attention? She's out for revenge."

"Alice is one woman against a whole town," Carmody said. "She doesn't stand a prayer."

"She's killed five men in an hour's time," Fargo said. "That's a damn good start." Climbing on the Ovaro, he flicked the reins.

"Why wasn't the marshal with them?"

"He's probably overseeing the search for the rest and sent Clyde and those other four after us."

"Too bad," Carmody said. "If he'd been with them, he'd be dead, too, and Alice would have her vengeance."

"You're forgetting the mayor and Gwendolyn and whoever else she's out to kill."

"You don't think—" Carmody stopped, as if her thought surprised her. "You don't think she's out to make the whole town suffer, do you? She wouldn't do something like poison their water, would she?"

"What makes you say that?"

"She mentioned a few times how much she hated the town and everyone in it. Said as how she'd like it if all of them were dead."

"Those were her exact words?"

"Pretty much."

"Damn."

"This is going to get a lot worse, isn't it?"

"A lot worse," Fargo predicted. He recollected how Alice had stood up to Deputy Brock in the barracks. At the time he'd thought she had spunk. Now he saw her defiance as a vein that ran deeper and darker. "Do you have a friend who could put you up for a while?"

"Excuse me?" Carmody said.

"Somewhere you can lie low while I hunt for her."

Carmody considered and said, "There's Jugs. You said you know her, didn't you?"

"Yes," Fargo said. He didn't expand on how or what Jugs had done in court.

"She'll help me if anyone will. But we'll be seen riding in."

"Not if we wait until dark."

The sun was well on its downward arc when Fargo veered into a stand of trees. As he swung down, his leg brushed his empty rifle scabbard. "Damn her," he said.

In the distance loomed Fairplay.

"I wish there was some other way," Carmody said.

"You can wait here."

"With nothing to eat or drink?" She waved a hand, dismissing the notion. "No, thanks. I like a roof over my head at night. I'm fond of a soft bed. I'd rather stay with Jugs."

Fargo leaned against an oak and folded his arms.

"I've been meaning to ask. How far are you willing to take this?"

"Far?" Fargo said.

"Let's say you find her. What then? You ask her, pretty please, that she give back your rifle and come with us? What if she won't? What if she's hell-bent on killing? How far are you willing to go to stop her?"

"As far as I have to."

In not quite an hour, bright reds and yellows and a splash of orange lit the western sky as the last sliver of sun was about to set.

Fargo took out his Colt. Normally he kept the chamber

under the hammer empty, but he added a sixth cartridge. Something told him he'd need it, and more, before this was over.

A canopy of stars twinkled overhead when he once more climbed on the stallion.

Carmody was slow to do the same. "Any chance you'd change your mind?"

"No."

"What's so special about this damn rifle?"

"It's mine."

"That's it?"

"That's enough," Fargo said, "when she's using it to kill."

"Last I heard, that's what rifles are for."

"Give it a rest," Fargo said in annoyance.

To his relief, she did.

Staying clear of the road, they rode on.

"Do you hear that?" Carmody asked.

Fargo did. Shouts and whoops, as if a celebration were taking place. The racket was punctuated by a few shots.

"What the hell?"

Fargo didn't know what to make of it, either. One thing was clear. They couldn't ride in until the town quieted down. He drew rein.

"Figures," Carmody said. "I'm dirty and hungry and thirsty. I need a bath and a hot meal. And I'm stuck out here with you."

"I know how we could spend the time," Fargo suggested with a grin.

"I'm not in the mood."

They sat their mounts in the growing cool of night as the sounds of mirth continued.

"They're having a grand time, whatever the hell they're doing," Carmody grumbled.

Fargo took a bundle wrapped in rabbit hide from his saddlebags and climbed down. "We might as well have supper."

"It's not jerky, is it? I don't like jerky much."

Fargo unfolded the hide and held out a piece. "This is pemmican."

She sniffed it and scrunched her face. "Did you make this yourself? What's in it?"

"Ground meat and fat and berries." Fargo bit and chewed, relishing the tangy taste.

"I'd rather go hungry."

Fargo was about to say, "Suit yourself," when he stiffened.

Hooves drummed. A single rider was on his way out of town, heading west.

Keeping low, Fargo darted to where he could see the road. He wondered if Mako had sent someone to check on the posse. A night ride made sense in that Comanches did most of their raiding during daylight.

An elbow bumped his. "Who is it?" Carmody wanted to know.

The rider appeared, a man much larger than most.

"Deputy Brock," Fargo suspected. His hunch had been right. He watched until the hoofbeats faded.

"Lucky you," Carmody said. "One less tin star you have to worry about."

Time crawled. So did the stars. It was pushing ten o'clock when the revelry died and Fairplay's usual quiet returned.

"About damn time," Carmody said.

They approached at a walk, Fargo with his hand on his Colt.

"It's not too late to change your mind," Carmody said hopefully as they neared the outskirts.

"You're like a dog with a bone," Fargo growled.

"I'm not hankering to die."

Nearly all the buildings were dark. A light glowed in the second-floor window of a house and in the Tumbleweed and another in the window of the marshal's office.

Concealed in black shadow at the end of the main street, Fargo surveyed it from end to end. He detected no evidence of an ambush.

He gigged the Ovaro. They went two blocks without incident.

In the distance a dog yapped and somewhere a woman was singing.

Up ahead, the saloon's batwings opened and out came a pair of townsmen.

Fargo quickly reined between a feed-and-grain and a butcher's.

Carmody wasted no time following him. "Do you think they saw us?"

Apparently not. The pair made off up the street in the other direction.

Fargo didn't budge until they were out of sight. "Keep your eyes skinned."

They'd only gone half a block more when Carmody whispered and pointed. "What's that?"

At first Fargo didn't see anything. Then he made out a hitch rail—and something else. It was too small for a horse, and it was under the rail instead of in front of it.

"What *is* that?" Carmody said again.

The short hairs at the nape of Fargo's neck prickled, but he couldn't say why.

They were almost to the hitch rail before they saw what it was. Both of them drew rein at the same instant and Carmody exclaimed, "God in heaven!"

16

It was one of the prisoners, stripped to the waist, his wrists lashed to the rail. His striped shirt lay in the dirt beside him.

Fargo didn't know the man's handle, but he remembered the face.

"That's Tilly!" Carmody gasped. "His real name was Tillson, but everyone called him Tilly."

The late Mr. Tillson had been shot between the eyes. Both had rolled up into his head, part of which was missing.

"Shot while trying to escape," was Fargo's guess.

"But why tie him to the rail like that?" Carmody asked, aghast. "How could they do such a thing?"

"A warning, maybe."

"To who?"

"The other prisoners."

"I bet it was the mayor's doing," Carmody said fiercely. "It's something he would do."

Fargo thought so, too.

Just then a loud *creak* caused both of them to stiffen.

"That sounded like a door," Carmody said.

It did to Fargo, too. After a couple of minutes went by and no one appeared, he said quietly, "I reckon it's safe enough," and clucked to the Ovaro.

"Safe, hell," Carmody said.

"You're going to make some hombre a fine nag someday," Fargo said.

"I get killed, I'm coming back to haunt you. I'll make your life miserable."

"You're off to a good start and you're not even dead yet."

"You're a coldhearted bastard—do you know that?"

"Says the woman who likes to bitch about everything."

Carmody let a few seconds go by and said, "But you do know how to please a lady." When he didn't respond she asked, "How about me? How was I for you?"

"I didn't fall asleep," Fargo said.

"You really are a bastard."

Fargo heard something but he wasn't sure what. He drew rein and listened. Other than the squall of a baby, the town lay undisturbed under the canopy of stars.

"What are we waiting for?" Carmody griped. "I don't like being out in the open."

Fargo was tired of her carping. The sooner he was shed of her, the sooner he could be about the business of finding Alice Thorn.

Sticking to side streets, he led her to Jugs's boardinghouse and on around to the rear.

Every window was dark.

"I just realized," Carmody whispered. "The doors are probably bolted. How will I get inside?"

"You'll see."

They dismounted.

Fargo opened the gate to the picket fence and Carmody followed him to the side of the house.

Fortunately, Jugs's room was on the ground floor. Fargo stood back and had Carmody tap on the window.

It took a while. At last the curtains parted and a face peered out and then fingers fumbled at the latch and the window scraped open.

"Carmody!" Jugs whispered in amazement. "Is that you?" She was wearing a nightdress that clung nicely to her breasts.

"I'm not alone," Carmody said. "I'm with a friend of yours."

Fargo moved to where Jugs could see him. "Remember me?"

Jugs's hand flew to her throat. "You!" she said. "It wasn't my fault. I had to testify the way I did."

"I saw the bruises," Fargo said. "Who beat you?"

"Deputy Brock," Jugs said. "At the marshal's bidding. He only hit me twice. It was enough." She looked from him to Carmody and out at the neighboring houses. "What are you doing here? I heard you got clean away."

"It's not my idea," Carmody assured her. "I need to lie low for a while and I was hoping you'd put me up. For old times' sake."

"It was wrong, what they did to you," Jugs said. "I raised a fuss about it and the mayor said if I kept on, he'd come up with something to charge me with and I could join you."

"I hate that son of a bitch more than I've ever hated anyone," Carmody said.

"You and me both. I suppose the smart thing for me to do was leave town, but I couldn't bring myself to do it with you behind bars."

Carmody clasped Jugs's hand. "I knew I could count on you."

"We always said we'd be friends forever," Jugs reminded her, her voice breaking.

"Ladies," Fargo interrupted. "Shed your tears inside, if you don't mind. I have a rifle to find."

"A rifle?" Jugs said.

"Don't ask," Carmody said as she hiked a leg to slide over the sill. "If dumb was money, he'd be rich."

Jugs helped her in and both bent and peered out.

"Something you should know," Jugs said. "They sent a posse after you."

"Their mistake," Fargo said.

"One other thing," Jugs said. "The marshal figures you

were to the blame for the escape, and the mayor was fit to be tied. I heard him mention how he plans to put a bounty on your head, dead or alive."

"The least of my worries," Fargo said.

"You won't think so when you hear how much. Five thousand dollars. Out of his own pocket, no less. He wants you to pay."

Fargo turned to leave.

"Something else," Jugs said. "Marshal Mako is out to nail your hide to a wall, too."

"He would be. He's the law."

"It's more than that. Mako thinks you made a laughing-stock of him, and he can't stand that."

"That's Skye for you," Carmody said. "He charmed me right out of my clothes."

"You, too?"

Fargo hurried around to the gate and the Ovaro. He took Carmody's mount with him since leaving it there might arouse suspicion.

By a circuitous route he reached an alley a block from the marshal's office. Swinging down, he stalked to where he could see the barracks.

A light glowed inside, and the padlock was back on the door.

Fargo crept to a barred window. More than half the men were in their bunks, their legs shackled. The rest had either gotten away or ended up like Tilly.

He moved to the last window.

Sarabeth was the only female. She was curled on her side with her blanket pulled as high as her ear.

On cat's feet Fargo stalked to the jail. The back door was open a crack. That surprised him. So did seeing the burly wagon driver named Travers slumped over the desk with his head cradled on his forearms, apparently asleep.

Gliding over, Fargo pressed the Colt's muzzle to his temple. "Rise and shine."

Travers didn't move, didn't react in any way.

Fargo rapped him with the barrel. "Wake up, lunkhead."

One of the man's arms slid out from under him, and his cheek hit the desk with a *thunk*.

"What the hell?"

Only then did Fargo see a crimson stain under Travers's chin. Blood so fresh, it glistened. He pressed a finger to Travers's neck to feel for a pulse.

"Don't bother," said a voice behind him as a gun was gouged against his spine. "I slit him from ear to ear. He's dead as dead can be."

"Alice?" Fargo said, knowing full well it was. He started to turn.

"Don't," she said, gouging harder.

"Is that my Henry?"

"It is."

"I want it back."

"Too bad. I've taken a shine to the thing. It's about the prettiest gun I ever did see. And it shoots as straight as can be."

"I'm not asking."

"Listen to you," Alice said. "I'm the one holding a gun on you, not the other way around."

"How about if I say 'please'?"

"How about if I say 'go play with yourself'?"

"Damn it all."

Alice motioned. "Set the six-gun down, step past the desk, and you can turn around."

Fargo did as she wanted, his arms out from his sides to show he wasn't a threat.

"That's far enough."

"Thank you for not shooting me," Fargo said.

"I haven't made up my mind yet what I'm going to do with you."

"You owe me."

"You're still breathing, ain't you? That counts for something right there."

Fargo nodded at the marshal's gun cabinet. "Take one of Mako's rifles and give me mine and I'll go my way and leave you to your killing."

"I just told you," Alice said, "I've taken a shine to it."

"You'd steal my rifle after I helped you get away?"

"There's more to this than you and me."

"You're as pigheaded as they come," Fargo said in disgust.

"And proud of it."

Fargo gestured at the body. "What does that make? Six you've killed since I freed you? How many more before you're happy?"

"Everyone who had a hand in putting me behind bars is going to die."

"All I ask if that you don't do it with my Henry. That's fair, isn't it?"

"What does fair have to do with anything?" Alice sat on the edge of the desk, the Henry rock-steady in her hands. "You need your ears cleaned out. I'm keeping your rifle and that's final."

"There's a Spencer in the cabinet." Fargo could see it from where he stood. "It's as good as my Henry. Why not take that?"

"Maybe it is as good. Maybe it ain't." Alice paused. "And maybe you don't care that they arrested you and put you on trial and were set to lock you away for a good long spell."

"I damn well do."

"Not enough, or you'd savvy why I can't leave it be. Where I come from we stomp our own snakes."

"I admire that, girl, but—"

"I'm not no *girl*. I'm a full-grown woman. Would that I weren't." Alice looked down at herself. "It's partly why I left home and was on my way to visit my aunt. I hankered to see more of the world than the farm fields of east Texas. Is that so wrong?"

"You're full-grown," Fargo acknowledged. "Act your age, then."

Alice snorted. "I'm being childish because I stand up for myself?"

Fargo tried one more time. "All I want is my rifle. Please."

"I didn't take you for a weak sister, but I reckon I was mistaken." Alice gnawed her bottom lip. "Still, you did break me out. So I reckon I'll give you a choice. We can do this easy or hard."

"What's the easy?"

"I lock you in that cell yonder so you can't interfere."

"And the hard?"

"I blow your brains out."

"That's your idea of being fair?"

"No." Alice Thorn smiled. "It's my way of saying thank you."

17

Fargo didn't doubt she'd splatter his brains. Look at how many she'd killed already. But he still balked.

"You put me in that cell and Mako will slap a chain on me. I can't have that."

"And I can't have you trying to stop me from doing what needs doing."

"You say you owe me for breaking you out," Fargo said. "How about this, then? You walk away and I don't try to stop you."

"What about later on?"

"All bets are off."

Alice scrunched up her face in thought. "I wouldn't want you in chains because of me. I wouldn't wish that on a dog. But I don't like the notion of having to look over my shoulder from here on out, either."

"You'll have to anyway," Fargo said. "Mako will be after you as soon as he finds out about the posse and what you did here."

An odd little grin quirked Alice's lips. "Will he, now?" Stepping back, she lowered the Henry but kept it trained on him. "All right. I won't lock you up. But mark my words. You try to stop me, I'll put lead in you."

"One thing," Fargo said.

"You can't change my mind, so don't bother trying."

"Not that," Fargo said, and nodded at the Henry. "My rifle. I still want it back."

"Damn, you are stubborn."

"Take another from the gun rack and leave mine on the floor."

"We've already been through this."

"It's mine," Fargo said.

"Not anymore. I reckon I'll hold on to it."

"Damn it, Alice."

"Don't be cussing me. I could have shot you a minute ago and didn't. How about we swap your life for your rifle? That's a fair trade."

"You leave my rifle and I'll leave you be."

Alice shook her head and began backing toward the rear door. "Sorry. The last rifle I owned was a single-shot squirrel gun. It wasn't shucks compared to this one."

"Stealing my rifle is the same as stealing my horse," Fargo said, trying to impress on her why he couldn't let it drop.

"No, it's not," Alice responded, "and be thankful I don't take your stallion, too. He's a mighty fine animal."

"I never would have guessed you're such a bitch."

"That's the way," Alice said, and laughed. "Sweet-talk me." She reached the door and paused. "Let this be the last time I set eyes on you."

"It won't be."

"From here on out I won't be as nice. For your own sake, ride off while you can."

"Any other time, I'd admire your grit," Fargo admitted.

"No doubt about it," Alice said. "You have a sugarcoated tongue." She grinned and winked and melted into the darkness.

In a bound Fargo scooped up his Colt and ran to the back door. Careful not to show himself, he peered out.

Alice Thorn had disappeared.

Fargo swore. He wondered who she would go after next, the marshal or the mayor. He didn't know where Mako lived, so that left His Honor.

He hurried to the Ovaro and rode at a trot to the north end of town. Once in the open, he came to a gallop.

The sky was an indigo vault lit by a host of sparkling stars.

A meteor cleaved the canopy, leaving a fiery trail in its wake.

Fargo recollected hearing that some folks regarded shooting stars as bad omens. Fortunately he wasn't superstitious.

He passed countless cows, dim bulks off in the murk. Most were lying down.

At the turnoff he stopped.

The ranch house was as dark as the rest of the world. All was still, save for a slight breeze.

Fargo headed up the lane. Midway he reined wide to a stand of trees not far from the stable. It was as good a spot as any to lie low until Alice showed up.

He'd meant what he said about admiring her grit. She had more sand than most men.

He hoped to God he could get his rifle back without her forcing him to do something he didn't want to do.

He didn't give a damn about the marshal and the mayor. As far as he was concerned, she could blow out their wicks, and good riddance.

The stand was small, but it would do. He slid down and looped the reins around a sapling and moved out into the grass where he could watch the house and the road.

Now all he could do was wait.

Fargo pushed his hat back, and stretched. He could use some sleep. And a bottle of whiskey. And to be hell gone from Fairplay.

He tiredly rubbed his eyes. When he opened them, he caught movement near the stable.

Two dark forms, low to the ground, were gliding into the grass.

Dogs.

Fargo debated running to the Ovaro and fanning the

breeze, but if they came after him, they'd go for the stallion's legs and might bring it down.

Instead he slid the Arkansas toothpick out.

They didn't bark, which was strange. They didn't even growl, which was stranger. Swift and silent, they streaked in with their fangs bared and their hackles bristling.

Fifty to sixty pounds each, Fargo guessed, with stocky, powerful bodies, and thick legs. And they were coming for the kill.

Fargo crouched.

The first dog didn't slow, didn't hesitate. It sprang and its mouth gaped wide to rip and rend.

In a blur, Fargo slashed its neck and swiveled aside. Wet drops spattered as the dog went past.

It didn't yelp or growl.

Fargo had no time to wonder why. The second dog was on him. It didn't spring. It hurtled at his legs, apparently intending to bowl him over. He jumped straight up, or tried to. His bootheels caught on the dog's shoulders.

Upended, Fargo sprawled to the ground. He heaved to his knees and went to stand, but it was too late.

The dogs were on him again.

Fargo stabbed a hairy chest and nearly cried out as teeth sheared into his right shoulder. The dog's jaws clamped and held fast. He stabbed it in the face.

The other dog lunged at his belly and he backhanded it.

The first dog still clung to his shoulder. He stabbed it again, in the eye, and the dog let go and jerked back, tossing its head.

The second dog bored in. He cut its muzzle and, when it recoiled, cut its neck.

Both dogs retreated but only a short way.

The reprieve bought Fargo time to heave to his feet. He couldn't get over how the pair didn't make a sound no matter what he did. He wondered if they had been trained that way and then wanted to kick himself for thinking about something so ridiculous when he should be thinking about what really mattered: staying alive.

The dogs looked at each another and attacked simultaneously.

Fargo sliced high, thrust low. He drove them back but only a few steps.

In the starlight their eyes seemed to blaze with demonic light.

They were smart, these dogs. They couldn't get at him head-on, so one began to circle to the left and the other to the right.

"Damn."

Something about his voice gave them momentary pause. They held still until one gnashed the air with its teeth, breaking the spell.

Fargo backpedaled to keep them from closing in from both sides at once, but they stayed with him, their heads tilted low, their fangs glistening like small sabers.

He thought he heard a noise from the direction of the house, but he dared not look away. The dogs would be on him in a heartbeat.

The dog on the left stopped and stared at the dog on the right. The dog on the right stopped and both of them crouched.

Fargo braced his legs to keep from being bowled over. He needn't have bothered. Neither attacked low; both brutes leaped at his neck and face. He drove the toothpick into one and slammed the second with a fist.

They retreated once more.

Fargo yearned to use the Colt. He could finish this with two shots. But it would rouse whoever was in the house and, worse, alert Alice to his presence if she was anywhere around.

The dogs pounced, their movements so well coordinated that they moved as one.

Fargo winced at a stinging sensation in his left leg. He

lanced the toothpick into a neck and whirled toward the other just as its teeth closed on his wrist. Images of his blood spraying every which way and of bleeding to death there in the tall grass flashed through his mind, even as he rammed the toothpick to the hilt.

Suddenly his arm was free. He took several quick steps back.

Both dogs were down. One was motionless, but the other convulsed in a violent spasm that ended with it flat on its back with its paws clawing at the sky. Then it, too, went limp.

Fargo sank to his knees. He was hurting, and bleeding. His wrist had a few bite marks, but they weren't deep. His shoulder, though, could stand to be bandaged.

Rising, he turned to go into the trees. He had an old buckskin shirt he could cut into strips for bandages.

It was under the bundle of pemmican. He changed his mind and cut the rabbit hide, instead. Tying it one-handed proved awkward, but he managed.

What Fargo wouldn't give for some whiskey. He'd stopped most of the bleeding, but the pain was worse. He'd just have to grit his teeth and bear it.

It occurred to him that he'd just made it easier for Alice Thorn. With the dogs disposed of, she could easily slip into the house and have her revenge.

"Some days," Fargo said to the Ovaro. He replaced his spare shirt and what was left of the rabbit hide.

Wheeling, he strode toward the house with the toothpick in his left hand.

He was out of the trees and had taken several steps when the grass rustled and a gun hammer clicked behind him. He turned his head and was face-to-muzzle with a rifle. "Well, now," he said. "Out for a late-night stroll?"

"You just killed our dogs, you son of a bitch. Get set to meet your Maker."

18

Fargo had expected His Honor. Or maybe a hired hand. Instead it was a vision of loveliness with grim death on her face.

No doubt about it, Gwendolyn Stoddard was a beauty. She wore a robe that even in the starlight highlighted her ample charms. Every contour, every swell, was a feast for the eye. The same starlight lent a shimmering luster to her golden hair and her eyes with green fire.

"I'd love to lick you all over," Fargo said, moving the toothpick behind his leg so she wouldn't notice it.

Jerking her head up from the rifle, Gwen responded, "What was that?"

"Lick," Fargo said, "you."

"I'm holding a gun on you and that's what you say?"

"Any chance?" Fargo said.

Gwen shook her head as if she couldn't believe her ears. "*You just killed our dogs.*"

"They were trying to kill me."

"They were guard dogs," Gwen declared angrily. "We set them loose every evening to keep watch."

"Then it's your fault they're dead."

"Mine?" Gwendolyn exploded. "You have your nerve. I should shoot you where you stand."

"A chip off the old block."

"What are you talking about? My father has never shot anyone."

"No," Fargo said. "He has his shooting done for him."

"If you're referring to the marshal and his deputies, the only shooting they do is in carrying out their official duties."

"That, and tying people they've killed to hitch rails," Fargo said.

"That man got what was coming to him. He'd escaped from custody and resisted when Marshal Mako tried to take him in."

"His fists against Mako's guns?" Fargo said. "How fair was that?"

"I don't know if he was unarmed. What does it matter? He shouldn't have resisted arrest." Gwendolyn paused. "What are you doing here, anyhow? I would have thought you'd be long gone by now."

"If it was up to me I would be."

"Try making sense for once."

"I'm after my rifle."

"What are you doing here? We sure as hell don't have it."

"Alice Thorn does."

"Thorn?" Gwen said. "Why is that name familiar?" Her brow puckered. "Wait a minute. I know her. She's done work out here. She's one of those who escaped."

"And she's out for blood. So far she's killed two deputies and others."

"Killed them? Why?"

"An eye for an eye. I think she aims to give your pa her regards next."

"My God. You're serious? And what? You expect me to believe that you're here to stop her?"

"I'm here for my rifle."

"That's all?"

Fargo gave her a hungry look, and grinned. "Unless I get to lick you."

"Stop with the licking. We have to warn my father."

"Not me," Fargo said, sliding his right foot forward. "I'd just as soon he rot in hell."

"I happen to think highly of him. He lives and breathes law and order."

"Is that what you call having folks arrested on trumped-up charges and putting them in chains?" Fargo took another half a step.

"My father never convicts anyone who doesn't deserve it."

"Tell that to Alice Thorn."

"Surely you're not comparing her to him?"

"They have a lot in common." Fargo stalled while moving his other foot. Soon he would be close enough.

"She's a criminal. A murderer, if I remember. My father was elected mayor and appointed himself judge because he didn't trust anyone else to do the job as well as he can."

Fargo snorted—and took yet another step.

"Enough talk," Gwen said. "Put your hands in the air. I'm taking you inside and we'll send for the marshal."

"Whatever you say," Fargo said. He started to raise his arms and as he did he tossed the Arkansas toothpick to the ground at her feet. She did what most anyone would have done: she took a quick step back and stared at the knife.

A single bound, and Fargo had hold of her rifle. Wrenching it from her grasp, he smiled. "That was plumb easy."

"No!" Gwendolyn cried, and tried to snatch it back.

Thrusting his left foot behind her legs, Fargo swept them out from under her. She squawked and landed hard on her backside. Covering her, he scooped up the toothpick and slid it into his ankle sheath.

Gwendolyn squirmed and rubbed her bottom. "That was mean. I won't be able to sit for a week."

"On your feet." Fargo scanned the buildings and the lane but saw no sign of anyone. Apparently Alice Thorn had yet to arrive.

"What do you intend to do with me?"

"Save your hide, if I can."

"And my father?"

"I already told you he can rot in hell for all I care." Fargo meant it. Horatio Stoddard was as big a bastard as he'd ever come across. He wouldn't lose a minute's sleep if Alice Thorn were to put a slug between Stoddard's eyes.

"Well, I care," Gwen said. Rising, she adjusted and smoothed her robe. "I won't stand by and let anyone harm him. Not you, and certainly not that Thorn woman."

Fargo was about to order her to get moving when he glimpsed a figure near the darkened house. "Is someone else up?"

"There's just my father and me, and he was sound asleep when I came out. I heard him snoring."

"Then it's her," Fargo said. Grabbing Gwendolyn's wrist, he pulled even as he broke into a run.

"What are you doing?"

"How did you know I was out here?" Fargo asked, intent on the figure.

"Oh." Gwen puffed her cheeks out as she sought to keep pace. "My bed is next to my window. When I can't sleep I like to just lie there and look out and—" She stopped and whispered, "Who's that?"

Fargo had seen the same thing: a figure moving along the side of the ranch house. Halting, he yanked her down beside him.

"Is that her?"

"Odds are."

They were about forty feet from the house. Fargo didn't think the figure had spotted them.

"Why have we stopped? Let's jump her."

"You don't shut up," Fargo warned, "I'll shut you up."

The figure reached the rear and peered around the corner. Something long and bright gleamed in the figure's hands.

Fargo's Henry. He went to turn to Gwen to tell her to stay put.

"You there!" she hollered unexpectedly. "Who are you and what are you doing here?"

At her shout, the figure whirled. The gleaming object rose.

Fargo dived, hauling Gwendolyn with him. He wasn't a moment too soon. The night rocked to three swift shots, and lead buzzed over their heads. He snapped off a shot with Gwen's rifle, but the figure was already in motion, racing back the way it came.

"Damn you," Fargo growled. Pushing up, he gave chase.

"Stop!" Gwen yelled at the shooter.

The figure—it had to be Alice Thorn—was running like a bat out of hell. She reached the front and slipped out of sight.

Mentally cussing a mean streak, Fargo reached the same spot and stopped. He poked his head out and the Henry blasted, the slug nicking his hat. Dropping flat, he took the hat off and eased an eye to the corner. There was no sign of Alice. He waited, hoping she would show herself. But the minutes dragged and she didn't.

Unexpectedly, there was a sound behind him.

Twisting, Fargo pointed the rifle and did more swearing.

"What are you so mad about?" Gwen whispered, crawling up next to him.

Fargo decided it wouldn't help matters to call her a stupid damn cow. He settled for saying, "You should have listened."

"It's my father in there," Gwen said. "Why can't you get that through your head?" She tried to crawl past him.

Clamping a hand on her shoulder, Fargo said, "Do you want your fool head shot off?"

"Where is she?"

"I don't know."

"Are you sure it was her?"

"As sure as I can be."

"You don't inspire much confidence."

"And you don't know when to shut the hell up."

Even in the dark, Fargo saw her color with indignation.

"No one has ever talked to me the way you do."

"Spoiled daddy's girl, is why."

"Why, you . . . ," Gwen said, and cocked an arm to punch him.

From out of the tall grass between the house and the road came a shout from Alice Thorn.

"Fargo? Is that you?"

Surprised, Fargo sought some sign of her.

"Why don't you answer?" Gwen whispered.

Alice Thorn had a question of her own. "Why couldn't you leave it be? He has to be put down or else it will go on and on."

Fargo frowned.

"You know I'm right, don't you?" Alice shouted. When he still didn't respond, she called out, "If this is how you want to be, fine. From here on out I'll consider you on their side. It's a shame you're so pigheaded."

"She sure knows you," Gwen said.

Fargo cupped a hand to his mouth. "Alice!" he yelled. She didn't reply. He yelled her name a second time with the same result.

"What did you expect? You didn't answer her. Why should she answer you?"

"I wonder," Fargo said.

"What she'll do next?"

"Whether pistol-whipping you would do any good."

"You wouldn't," Gwendolyn gasped.

"No, he won't," a new voice declared behind them.

Fargo turned, and this time found himself staring up into a shotgun.

19

Fargo froze. He was tired of having guns pointed at him, but he wasn't about to move a muscle with the business end of a hand cannon trained on his face.

"What the hell is going on out here, daughter?" Horatio Stoddard demanded. He, too, wore a robe, only his was bulky and ill-fitting. His thin hair, normally slicked back, stuck out at all angles. "I was roused out of a deep sleep by shots and shouting."

Quickly rising, Gwendolyn said, "It's Fargo."

"I can see that," Horatio snapped. "Who else is out there? Who was he yelling to?"

"That woman who escaped," Gwendolyn said. "Alice Thorn. She killed the men in the posse and now she's out to kill us."

"Preposterous," Horatio said. "She's a snip of a woman. And she hasn't given us any trouble since she was sentenced. Unlike that Carmody Wells."

"But I heard her," Gwendolyn said, "and she took shots at us."

"Perhaps it was a ruse to draw us out," Horatio suggested.

"Shouldn't we get inside, then?"

"Excellent suggestion. Take the rifle from him, and his six-gun." To Fargo Horatio said, "And you, sir. Give me any excuse and I will blow you apart."

Gwendolyn dutifully relieved Fargo of the rifle and

plucked the Colt from his holster. "Now you're in for it," she gloated, and laughed.

Horatio stepped back. "On your feet. Hands in the air."

Left with no recourse, Fargo complied. He gauged the distance but didn't spring.

"Now, then," Horatio said, "we'll escort you inside and bind you and I'll get word to Marshal Mako. Need I stress that any act on your part I deem threatening will result in your immediate demise?"

"I came here to stop here to stop Alice Thorn," Fargo said.

"And I'm infantile enough to believe that," Horatio said, sneering. "It makes perfect sense you'd want to save my life after I'd sentenced you to years behind bars."

Gwendolyn laughed.

"No, what we have here," Horatio went on, "is you out for our blood. If it's true the posse members are dead, then it was your doing, not Alice Thorn's."

"Jackass."

Horatio put his cheek to the shotgun. "That's right. Incite me to anger. Were I not so law-abiding, I'd drop you where you stand."

"Maybe you should anyway," Gwendolyn said. "He killed both our dogs."

"He did what?"

Fargo tensed. With the judge in front of him and the daughter behind him, there wasn't much he could do, but he wouldn't stand there meekly and be shot down.

"Killed our poor dogs," Gwendolyn said, and jabbed Fargo in the back with his own Colt.

"I can't wait to get him in court," Horatio told her. "Between his escape and this attempt on our lives, I can sentence him to life."

"That would be fitting."

"Bitch," Fargo said.

"Enough!" Horatio barked. "Walk around to the front

door. No tricks. And keep your arms up where I can see them."

Fargo resigned himself to doing as he was told, for the time being. He half expected Alice Thorn to open fire on them, but apparently she was no longer out there.

Gwen opened the door and the judge gave Fargo a shove. "In you go."

It was all Fargo could do to contain his anger. A wide hall brought him to a parlor.

"On the settee," Horatio commanded.

"I'll fetch rope," Gwen volunteered, and scooted off.

"She's a good girl, that Gwendolyn," Horatio said proudly. "Takes after her mother."

"Haven't seen her yet," Fargo said.

"My Maude died giving birth to Gwen," Horatio revealed. "I've had to raise her on my own. With the help of seven or eight nannies."

"Seven or eight?"

"They have a habit of quitting on me. I'm too demanding, they say."

"Imagine that."

Horatio's thin lips creased in a sinister smile. "I intend to give Marshal Mako considerable latitude in dealing with you."

"Use little words," Fargo said.

"Were he to beat you within an inch of your life, I wouldn't reprimand him."

"Don't you ever get tired of being such a bastard?"

Rage twisted Horatio's face, but he regained his composure and said, "A bastard with *power*. You'd do well to remember that."

"When the governor finds out what you're up to," Fargo said, "he'll put a stop to it."

"First it was the army. Now it's the governor. You truly do clutch at straws." Horatio chortled in amusement.

"You'll be laughing out your ass once Carmody Wells gets to Austin."

"What's that you're saying?"

"Carmody Wells," Fargo lied glibly. "She went to Austin to report you to the governor. With your posse dead, she has a good chance of getting through."

For a few moments Horatio appeared worried, but then he shook his head. "Do you really think Governor Clark will believe the word of a common trollop?"

"I sent a letter with her to back her story," Fargo said.

"I very much doubt that the governor knows you from Adam."

"I met him once. He'll remember me."

A hint of worry crept into Horatio's expression. "Damn me if I don't think you're telling the truth."

Fargo smiled.

"The last thing I need is busybodies from the state government snooping around. They might not agree with my methods."

"There's more," Fargo said, piling the manure on. "I told her to get in touch with all the kin she can of the men you have in that barracks of yours."

"You didn't."

"Anything to make your life miserable," Fargo said.

Horatio grew livid and made as if to shoot but jerked the shotgun down. "No. I'd better not. On the off chance your governor story is true."

Fargo was a good poker player for a reason; relief washed over him, but it didn't show.

"Damn, damn, damn."

Gwendolyn returned carrying two lengths of rope. "Here we go," she said.

"Tie him while I cover him and then you're heading for town," Horatio informed her. "I need Marshal Mako out here right away."

"You expect me to ride all the way to town alone? In the middle of the night? With that madwoman out there?"

"Fine," Horatio snapped. "I'll go. Just hurry and bind him."

Fishing for information, Fargo remarked, "Don't you have ranch hands you can send?"

"The prisoners do all the work I need done. I save a lot of money that way."

"As sons of bitches go," Fargo said, "you're near the top of the heap."

"Quit talking about him that way," Gwen said.

She had Fargo put his arms behind his back and wrapped a rope around his wrists and knotted it. Kneeling, she was about to do the same with his ankles, but stopped.

"What's the matter?" Horatio asked.

"I just remembered." Hiking Fargo's pant leg, Gwen slid her fingers down his boot and relieved him of the Arkansas toothpick. "I saw him with this earlier."

"Good girl," Horatio said. "He's devious, this one."

Once she had the second rope tight, Gwendolyn stepped back. Her father handed her the shotgun and left to get dressed.

Leaning against the wall, Gwen held the shotgun in the crook of an elbow and grinned like a cat that was playing with a canary. "I reckon you wish you'd never set eyes on Fairplay."

"You should change the name to something that fits," Fargo said. "Shitplay, maybe. Or Locoland."

"Funny man," Gwen said. Now that he was at her mercy, she was relaxed and in better spirits.

Without being obvious, Fargo tested the rope around his wrists. She'd done a good job. It would take considerable doing to work his hands free.

"It's too bad how things worked out," Gwen remarked. "I sort of liked you. You're about the handsomest fella I ever did see."

Fargo grunted.

"Truth to tell," she rambled on, "I wouldn't have minded a frolic."

"We still can," Fargo said.

"You honestly expect me to untie you so we can do *that*?"

"How about if I give my word I won't try and run off?" Fargo said.

"You must think I'm as dumb as a rock."

"I think you're a peach, and I'd like to suck on you until you gush in my mouth."

"There you go again," Gwen said. Damned if she didn't blush. "Not another word about that, you hear?"

From overhead came the clomp of boots.

"I'll say one thing for you," Gwen informed him. "You've given my father and the marshal more trouble than anyone ever has."

"I'm just getting started."

She laughed and motioned at his bound legs. "I love an optimist."

They were silent after that.

In a few minutes Horatio returned, dressed in the long coat and hat he usually wore, only this time with the addition of a revolver strapped around his waist. On him it looked ridiculous. "I'm leaving," he announced.

"Don't take too long," Gwen said.

"And don't you go near him until I return. No matter what."

"I wouldn't think of it."

"I mean it, daughter. Control those urges of yours." Horatio didn't wait for her to reply but wheeled and headed down the hall.

"Be careful," Gwen called after him.

Fargo sighed and sat back. He idly glanced at a window, and froze.

A face stared back in, twisted with hate.

The face of Alice Thorn.

20

The face was there and then it was gone.

Fargo realized she hadn't been glaring at him. Her hate was directed at Gwendolyn Stoddard. "You might want to let me loose."

Gwen was moving toward an easy chair, and stopped. "Why on earth would I?"

"Alice Thorn."

"Is long gone." Gwendolyn sat and placed the shotgun across the chair's arms. Leaning back, she smothered a yawn. "I'll need an extra-long nap later today to make up for the sleep I've lost." She fluffed her hair and ran a hand over a cheek. "I nap daily. It's the secret to a smooth complexion."

"What's the secret to not being shot?"

"You never quit, do you? That Thorn woman isn't about to march in here and shoot me. I had nothing to do with her arrest and imprisonment."

"I'll ask you once more." Fargo felt compelled to try. "Set me free before it's too late."

Gwendolyn laughed. "You sure are polite when you grovel."

They both heard the drum of hooves.

"There goes my father," Gwen said.

Fargo waited for the blast of a shot. None came. He wondered why Alice didn't pick Horatio off as he was riding away. It would be easy, even in the dark. He had a suspicion as to why she hadn't, and it suggested a lot worse yet to come.

Gwen said happily, "By morning you'll be behind bars again where you belong."

"By morning you might be dead."

Gwen frowned and smacked the shotgun in irritation. "That's enough. Talk about something else. I'm tired of you trying to scare me into untying you."

A slight breath of cool air fanned Fargo's face. He turned his head toward the hall and it became stronger. "You should at least have bolted the front door."

Gwen let out a loud sigh. "Will you *please* give it a rest? Nothing is going to happen."

Alice Thorn stepped into the parlor and pointed the Henry at Gwendolyn Stoddard. "Care to bet?"

Gwen gasped and had the good sense not to try to raise the shotgun. "You!"

"Why are you so surprised?" Alice asked. "I heard him warn you, but you wouldn't listen." She looked at Fargo. "I should shoot you for that, but I reckon I won't."

"What do you want?" Gwen demanded.

Alice moved toward her, her thumb curled around the Henry's hammer, her finger around the trigger. "Pretend you don't know."

"I honestly don't."

"Of course not," Alice said. "All you care about is yourself." She carefully took the shotgun and stepped back and propped it against the wall well out of Gwendolyn's reach.

"Are you going to hurt me?"

"I'm about to do a hell of a lot more than hurt," Alice said.

Fargo cleared his throat to get her attention and said simply, "Don't."

"Stay out of this," Alice said.

"She had no hand in it. It was her father and the marshal."

"Mostly," Alice said. "But this one"—and she glared at

Gwen—"with her high-and-mighty airs. You never saw what she did. How she acted."

"I never did anything to you," Gwen said.

"You didn't do anything *for* me, either, bitch." Alice's mouth became a slit. "All the times we were brought out here to work on your ranch. The men broke their backs digging ditches and shoveling manure and doing all the other dirty jobs your pa thought up."

"I never once had those men, or you women, do a thing for me," Gwen said.

"No, it was always your pa. It was him had us sweep your floors and clean your windows and take out your garbage. It was him had us make your goddamn bed and wash your goddamn clothes and hang them out to dry on the goddamn line. It was him who had us empty your stinking chamber pots."

"Then why are you so mad at me?"

"Because," Alice said, her whole body shaking with the intensity of her emotions, "you never once told him he shouldn't. You never one said it wasn't right to have us act like your slaves."

"Oh, please. Now you're exaggerating. If you'll recall, my father didn't let me anywhere near you when you were out here. You were always under guard by one of the deputies."

"You walked past us a hundred times or more and never so much as looked our way. You treated us like we weren't even there."

"I was supposed to."

"And when it comes to what your pa wants, you kiss his ass."

Gwen gripped the chair's arms so tight that her knuckles were white. "You little no-account bitch. If you weren't holding that rifle on me, I'd show you a thing or two."

"Oh, really?"

To Fargo's surprise, Alice Thorn propped the Henry

against the wall next to the shotgun and moved over in front of the chair.

"Show me, then."

"You just made a big mistake," Gwen said, looking the smaller woman up and down with undisguised contempt.

"I'm waiting."

Rising, Gwen balled her fists. She towered over Alice by a good foot and a half and had to outweigh her by thirty to forty pounds. "I'll pound you into the floor."

"Start pounding," Alice said, and drove her right hand up, palm flat, into Gwen's jaw.

From across the room Fargo heard the *crack* of Gwen's teeth smashing together. The blow knocked her into the chair and she sat there with her eyes half-glazed, blinking in confusion. Blood trickled from her mouth and down over her chin.

"I'm still waiting," Alice Thorn said, taking several steps back.

With a toss of her head, Gwendolyn snapped out of her daze. She hissed like a bobcat and touched a finger to a drop of blood and stared at the scarlet smear. "I will by God kill you for that."

Alice glanced over at Fargo. "Windbag pa, windbag daughter."

A growl tore from Gwen's throat as she heaved out of the chair and threw herself at Alice Thorn with her fingers hooked like claws. "Kill you!" she shrieked.

Alice waited until the very last instant, until Gwendolyn was almost on top of her, to spin aside and ram her fist into Gwen's belly.

Gwen stopped as if she had hit a wall, and folded over. Spittle sprayed from her lips, along with the blood.

Smirking, Alice put her fists on her hips. "You're about as tough as a kitten."

Fargo was impressed. He'd been in more than his share of brutal slugfests. He'd tangled with men who used their fists as slickly as he used his Colt, and men who couldn't fight worth a lick. Alice Thorn could fight.

Gwen's hands were on her knees as she sucked in deep breaths. "You caught me by surprise," she said. "It won't happen twice."

Alice laughed, a peal of scorn that brought Gwen up in a fury. Gwen swung and Alice ducked. Gwen swung again and Alice blocked and landed two quick jabs to Gwen's chin.

Gwen backpedaled, stumbled, and almost went down. She managed to steady herself and held her open hands out toward Alice. "No more."

"Hell. I ain't begun to tear into you," Alice told her.

"Please," Gwen said. "You've hurt me enough."

Fargo saw fear on her face, heard fear in her voice. "You've punished her enough, Alice."

The freckled hellion whirled toward him, her face contorted in rage. "How the hell would you know what's enough? You weren't in chains. You weren't forced to lick their stinking boots day in and day out."

"I never—" Gwen started to say.

Alice whirled back around. "You never will again," she cried, and threw herself at the taller woman in a berserk fury.

Gwen tried to protect herself. She got her arms up, but Alice slammed two punches to her gut and when she doubled over, Alice rained blows on her face and neck.

Retreating under the onslaught, Gwen let out a piercing scream.

Fargo struggled against the ropes, to no avail. It was sickening to watch. Alice Thorn hit and hit and hit and all Gwen did was flail her hands.

"Stop! Please! I'm begging you!"

Alice did a remarkable thing; she hopped into the air and kicked Gwen full in the face. Gwen's nose crunched and more blood sprayed, and then she was on her back on the floor, thrashing and groaning.

Alice stood over her, revenge incarnate, blood on her knuckles and scarlet drops on her clothes.

"Enough, damn it," Fargo said.

Alice slowly straightened. She looked over at him and down at Gwendolyn. She looked at her fists and opened them and wiped them on her pants. She began to turn as if to walk away, but instead she suddenly let out a shriek of "Biittchhhhh!" and rammed her foot into Gwendolyn's ribs. Gwen cried out and attempted to crawl away as Alice kicked and kicked and kicked. Alice didn't stop until Gwen stopped moving.

"Happy now?" Fargo said bitterly.

Alice was trembling and breathing raggedly, and yet smiling. She wiped a bloody boot on Gwen's disheveled robe, then brought her heel down on Gwen's ear. There was another crunch.

A cold chill rippled down Fargo's spine. "Jesus," he breathed.

Alice went to the wall. She picked up the shotgun, broke it open, checked that both barrels were loaded, and snapped it shut. As she came back she pulled on both hammers.

The twin clicks were ominous.

"You're not," Fargo said.

"Tell them for me," Alice said, training the shotgun on Gwendolyn Stoddard's head. "Tell that bastard father of hers and that prick of a tin star that this is what's in store for them."

"Them, yes," Fargo said. "She doesn't deserve this."

"Like hell." Alice nudged Gwen with a toe. She had to poke several times before Gwen stirred sluggishly and opened her eyes.

"Damn it, no!" Fargo shouted.

"Can you see me, girl?" Alice asked.

"Yes," Gwen whined.

"Good," Alice Thorn said, and squeezed both triggers.

21

Fargo sat and stared at the ruin on the floor for he knew not how long. He heard Alice laugh as she moved to the hall, heard her say that he was lucky she was letting him live. She said she wanted to overtake Horatio before he reached town and she gave a cheerful little wave and ran off.

She left the shotgun on the floor by what was left of Gwendolyn Stoddard's face and took his Henry.

Fargo had run into some cold killers from time to time. Outlaws, hostiles, men, and a few women who could kill anyone, anywhere, without batting an eye. But he'd never met one in so small and seemingly frail a package as this country girl who called herself Alice Thorn.

No one would ever suspect to look at her that she was as ruthless in her way as an Apache on the warpath.

The ticking of the grandfather clock brought him out of himself.

Sitting up, Fargo looked around. When Gwen tied him she'd taken his toothpick. It wasn't anywhere in the parlor. She'd had it in her hand when she went for rope, but she didn't have it when she'd returned.

Fargo rolled off the settee to the floor. He continued to roll to the hallway. Tucking his knees to his chest, he rolled to the kitchen. The smell of food hung in the air and made his stomach grumble.

A coiled rope hung on a peg by the back door. Probably the one Gwen had used, he reckoned.

Fargo didn't see his knife. He snaked over to a table and chairs. Sliding his legs under him, he lurched to his knees. By craning his neck he could see the top of the table.

"Found you," Fargo said. The toothpick was in the middle. Bracing his shoulder against a table leg, he shoved. The table shook and the knife rattled. He shoved harder with the same result.

Changing tactics, Fargo lay on his back and pressed the soles of his boots to the bottom. He gave a light push to test the weight. The table rose half an inch. Bunching his legs, he thrust up and out.

With a loud crash the table went over, taking a chair with it.

The Arkansas toothpick skittered across the floor and came to rest near the stove.

Fargo kicked a chair out of his way and rolled over to it. Within moments he had it in his hands and sliced at the rope around his wrists. The angle he had to hold it, it hurt like hell.

Gritting his teeth, he persisted. He kept the toothpick razor sharp, and the keen edge made short shrift of the strands.

The rope parted. He rubbed his wrists, then set to work on the loops around his ankles. In no time he was free. He slid the toothpick into its ankle sheath and stood.

The Colt was on a counter. He checked that it was loaded, twirled it into his holster, and was out the back door at a run.

The Ovaro was still in the trees.

Mounting, Fargo reined toward the road and used his spurs. He fully expected to come on Horatio Stoddard's body long before he reached Fairplay, but he didn't. At the edge of town he drew rein to ponder his next move.

Dawn was a couple of hours off yet.

The buildings were dark with a single exception, the streets quiet. The exception was the marshal's office. Two horses were at the hitch rail.

Fargo circled to a side street that would bring him to the rear. He never took his hand off his Colt. Alice was there, somewhere, and she'd made it plain she wouldn't let him stop her.

All Fargo had wanted was his Henry. If she'd given it to him, he wouldn't be there, wouldn't be risking his hide for two sons of bitches he'd as soon shoot himself.

The barracks was dark. The back door to the jail was closed.

His saddle creaking, Fargo alighted. He palmed the Colt.

From inside the barracks came loud snores.

From the office rose a loud voice.

Fargo put his ear to the door.

". . . hire you for?" Horatio Stoddard was saying angrily. "I don't care that your deputies have gotten themselves killed. I don't care that Brock's not back yet. I want you out at my house, and I want you out there *now*."

"He's trussed up, you said," Marshal Mako said. "And your gal has a gun on him. There's no hurry."

"Haven't you been paying attention? You're forgetting the Thorn girl."

"Maybe Fargo was lying about her," Mako said. "Maybe it was just him out there."

"My daughter thought different."

"We'll know for sure soon. Brock should be back any minute. We'll take him with us."

"I don't want to wait. Quit arguing or you'll find yourself out of a job."

"Was that a threat, Your Honor?" Luther Mako asked, and the way he said it was a threat in itself.

"Damn you," Horatio said. "It's my daughter we're talking about. Anything happens to her and I'll never forgive you."

"Relax," Mako said. "Ten minutes more, and I promise if Brock doesn't show, we'll light a shuck for your place."

"Ten goddamn minutes," Horatio said.

Fargo put his hand on the latch and was about to ease the door open when hooves thundered. A rider was coming down the main street hell-for-leather. The hoofbeats stopped in front of the jail and the front door crashed open.

"Marshal, you won't believe it!" Deputy Brock hollered.

"Calm yourself," Mako said.

"Wait," Brock said. "Is that Travers lying there by the cell?"

"The posse," Mako said. "Tell me about the posse."

"They're dead. Every last one. Clyde, too."

"How were they killed?"

"Shot. One each to the head or the heart."

"Then Fargo wasn't lying," Horatio Stoddard remarked.

"Or he shot them himself," Mako said.

"Enough dillydallying," Horatio snapped. "My daughter is alone with him. We're leaving right this minute."

"Someone want to tell me what's going on?" Deputy Brock said.

"We'll fill you in on the way," Marshal Mako said.

"What about the body?" Brock asked.

"It'll be here when we get back."

Fargo moved to the side of the jail and ran along it to the front but didn't show himself. If he did, Mako and the deputy were liable to cut loose with hot lead before he could explain.

The three emerged. The mayor stepped to the hitch rail and undid the reins to his mount.

Marshal Mako closed the door.

Brock gazed up and down the street and suddenly pointed across it and blurted, "Who's that yonder? I think they have a rifle."

Across the street an alley mouth rocked with the blast of shots.

Deputy Brock cried out and clutched his side.

Mayor Stoddard's horse whinnied and reared and wheeled to run off.

And in the blink of an eye, Marshal Luther Mako had both Starr revolvers in his hands and blazed away at the alley. He fired half a dozen shots faster than just about anyone Fargo had ever seen, and the shooting from the alley stopped.

"Inside!" Mako roared at the other two.

Brock needed no urging. He lurched at the doorway and plunged on through.

Horatio Stoddard, though, was rooted in consternation at the sight of his horse stumbling and then pitching to its front knees. "No!" he cried.

With surprising speed for his bulk, Marshal Mako darted to the mayor, shoved a pistol into a holster, grabbed Stoddard by the arm, and practically threw him at the doorway. Stoddard squawked and tripped and sprawled to the floor.

Retreating, Mako drew his holstered revolver and blasted four more shots at the alley. Another moment, and he was inside and the door slammed shut.

Fargo focused on the dark maw across the street. He was surprised Alice had stopped spraying lead. She could have picked off the mayor, easy.

Hunching low to the ground, he broke from cover and veered left. Braced for a hail of slugs, he zigzagged like mad. He reached the doorway to a barbershop without being shot at.

Puzzled, Fargo poked his head out and jerked it back again. Nothing happened. Either she hadn't noticed him crossing the street, which was unlikely, or she was no longer there.

Hoping he was right, Fargo dashed to the alley and flung himself flat. Once again no shots rang out.

The alley was as dark as the bottom of a well. Alice could be an arm's length away and he wouldn't know it.

Staying close to the building on the right to keep from silhouetting himself, Fargo stalked in. A third of the way in, he stopped and crouched and placed his left hand on the ground to balance himself. He nearly recoiled when he touched a wet spot. Raising his fingers, he sniffed his fingertips. The smell wasn't strong, but it was enough to tell him what it was.

Advancing, Fargo groped as he went. He found a few more wet spots.

The alley ended at the next street.

Clear in the starlight were glistening fresh drops on the plank walk.

Alice Thorn was bleeding.

Mako had hit her.

Fargo followed the drops. Twice he came on smudge marks where she'd stopped and turned to look back. She'd gone two blocks, crossed the street, and ducked into another alley.

Fargo risked a look-see. He saw nothing, heard nothing.

In his haste to catch up to her, he did something he shouldn't have done: he entered the alley without keeping low.

Almost immediately fireflies flared at the far end and leaden hornets sought to sting him. Fargo flattened, felt his hat whipped from his head, and answered twice with his Colt.

The shooting stopped.

Fargo stayed where he was. For effect he let out a groan. Let her think she'd hit him and she might come to see.

Long seconds went by, and from the other end of the alley, so weak he barely heard her, Alice Thorn called out, "Help me, please! I'm hurt bad."

22

Fargo heard her gasp and gurgle and a flurry of sounds that might be someone in their death throes. Then there was silence. Suspecting a trick, he stayed put. He found his hat and jammed it on.

A minute become two and two became three. He would have waited longer, but Luther Mako's hard tones from a block back spurred him to act.

"I tell you the shooting was around here somewhere. Keep looking until I say different."

"I shouldn't be doing this," Deputy Brock said. "I was shot, damn it."

"Hell, you were nicked, is all," Mako said in disgust. "Quit your blubbering, you damn big baby, and do as I tell you."

Rising, Fargo ran to the far end and stepped out, looking for Alice Thorn's body.

It wasn't there.

Fargo turned right and started to turn left, but a hard object was jammed against the base of his spine. "Hell," he said.

"I thought it was one of them or I wouldn't have shot at you," Alice said. "Drop the six-gun."

Frowning, Fargo opened his fingers and the Colt thudded to the ground.

"We both played the same trick and you took the bait," Alice said, scooping up the Colt.

"Like hell," Fargo said gruffly. "The marshal and his deputy are closing in."

"The big one?"

"Brock," Fargo confirmed.

"I thought I'd done him in. Nothing is going right tonight."

"Besides killing Gwen Stoddard," Fargo said.

"She had it coming. She was a party to it all." Alice sidled around, careful to keep out of his reach. She glanced into the alley. "I hear them."

So did Fargo. "Luther Mako won't be as easy as the others."

"That one's a he-wolf, sure enough," Alice said. "The only real killer of the bunch."

"Like you," Fargo said.

"You are so dumb, it's plumb pitiful," Alice said. She motioned with the Henry. "Head up the street that-away. We'll fetch my horse and then we'll fetch yours."

"We're going somewhere?"

"I won't have it be here," Alice said. "I know a nice place. I passed it when I first came to this godforsaken town." She motioned again. "Get moving."

Fargo was tempted to try and jump her. He thought of the posse and Travers and Gwen and decided to wait for a better chance.

"For the life of me, I can't figure why the Almighty let this happen," Alice remarked. "I was never much of a churchgoer, but I wasn't no sinner, neither."

"Good for you."

"You couldn't care less. I savvy that. It matters to me, though. Especially now."

"Why now?" Fargo asked.

Alice didn't answer, not right away. When she did, she had a question of her own. "Life sure is unfair, ain't it?"

"All the time," Fargo said.

"Look at Stoddard. As mean a bastard as ever drew

breath. Yet he lives in a fancy house and has a fine carriage and money to spare. How fair is that?"

Fargo was listening for the marshal and the deputy. They might distract her and he could get hold of the Henry.

"Why do you suppose God lets things be the way they are?"

"How the hell would I know?"

Alice didn't seem to hear him. "It starts out of the womb. Some babies live, some babies die. Those that live, some have it easy in life, some have it hard. Those that have it hard, it's not always their fault. They're poor, or sickly, or get kicked by a mule and their chest stove in."

"Why are we talking about this?"

"I'm making a point," Alice said. "But you're too stupid to see it." She gave a slight cough. "Walk faster, you turtle."

Her horse was tied to a hitch rail. She mounted, covered him, and had him lead her to the Ovaro. Twice they stopped when they heard searchers, but they weren't discovered.

"Where are you taking me?" Fargo asked after he forked leather.

"You'll see," Alice said. "It's a pretty spot. It'll do as good as any other."

She had him ride to the east edge of town. Once they were clear of the buildings, they bore to the south.

Open rangeland spread in a sea of grass that waved and rustled in the cool predawn breeze.

Soon the sun would rise. Already a pink tinge framed the eastern horizon.

"A right fine morning," Alice said.

Fargo grunted.

"Pick up the pace. I don't know how long it will be."

"To what?"

"Use those spurs of yours."

For the next couple of miles they held to a trot and then slowed.

"They're not far ahead now," Alice said. "Thank God."

Fargo didn't bother asking what she was referring to. She probably wouldn't say, anyway.

"You don't like me much, do you?"

"I don't like all the killing with my rifle."

"Not even if it's justified?"

"In your eyes," Fargo said.

"Mine are the ones that count."

After that she didn't speak again until a line of hills appeared. She scanned them and said, "Bear east a ways."

The hills formed a barrier between the rich grassland and rugged country beyond that eventually changed to miles of swamp bordering the gulf. Many of the hills were covered in trees and as picturesque as a painting.

Alice guided Fargo to one that was higher than most. The climb was easy enough. They drew rein on the clear crown and were treated to a panoramic vista that stretched in all directions for as far as the eye could see.

Alice breathed deep and smiled. "Didn't I tell you? Pretty as can be."

"You brought me all this way to admire nature?" Fargo said.

Alice sighed. "You gripe more than my grandma. Climb down, if you please. And even if you don't." Punctuating her demand, she pointed the Henry.

Fargo alighted and stretched and smothered a yawn. He'd been up all night and could use some sleep.

Dismounting, Alice gazed longingly into the distance. "I wish I could see it again. I wish it more than anything."

"See what?" Fargo asked, despite himself.

"My home. My ma and pa. My brothers and sisters. They warned me not to go traipsing off. But I wanted to see more of the world. Meet new people. Thought I'd visit my aunt first and you know how that went."

Fargo almost felt sorry for her. But he couldn't shake the sight of Gwen's head being blown to bits and pieces.

Alice pointed at a spot about ten feet from her. "Sit yonder."

"You enjoy bossing me around, don't you?"

"Gripe, gripe, gripe," Alice said. When he obeyed, she sank cross-legged, placed the Henry across her lap, and went on gazing wistfully into the distance.

"What now?" Fargo asked.

"We wait."

"For what?"

"You are a biddy hen in buckskins," Alice said, and grinned rather sadly.

"This just makes no damn sense."

"Ah," Alice said. "I reckon you have a right to know, seeing as how you'll have to tend to it, after."

"There you go again," Fargo said. "Talking in riddles."

"You gnaw at things like a dog with a bone," Alice said. Shifting slightly, she surprised him by commencing to unbutton her shirt. She undid the bottom four buttons, and winced.

"What's the matter?" Fargo said. "Are you in pain?"

"A light begins to dawn." Alice parted the shirt and raised it high enough for him to see her belly. Above it, just below the sternum, was a red-rimmed hole.

"Serves you right," Fargo said.

"That damned law dog can shoot. Put one in me quick as anything." She looked down at herself. "It went in and stayed. I think it rattled around in my ribs some. Hurts like the dickens."

Fargo didn't say anything.

Alice touched the bullet hole. "Hasn't bled much, has it? Wonder why that is."

Fargo stared at her and then out over the magnificent sweep of south Texas, and swore. "You came here to die."

"You're not as dumb as a stump, after all."

"Damn it. Why didn't you tell me?"

"What good would that do? You'd likely crab at me to see a sawbones. If I lived, the marshal would have me back in chains as soon as I was fit enough."

"You don't know that," Fargo said, fully aware that she was right.

"It's best this way. I die free. I die with my head high." Alice stopped and closed her eyes. In the growing light her freckles lent her a childlike quality. "I wanted so much to do them in for what they did to me."

"You'd gotten away," Fargo said. "There was no reason to go back other than pure hate."

"Think so, huh?" Her eyes still closed, Alice placed her hand over her belly and groaned.

Fargo could take her. He could be on her in a heartbeat and have the Henry. But he didn't move. "Alice?"

"I don't have long left. I can feel it." She raised her head and looked at him. "Three years of my life, and now this. That tin star will never know he killed two birds with one slug."

"Another riddle."

"If you were female you'd have already guessed."

Fargo stared at her belly and an awful realization crept over him. "Surely not," he said.

"Why he picked me I will never know." Alice rubbed her belly in small circles, a tear trickling from her eye. "Someone should know and it might as well be you."

"Hell, hell, hell," Fargo said.

"Finally figured it out, did you?" Alice stopped rubbing and a tear trickled from the other eye. "I'm pregnant."

23

For one of the few times in his life, Skye Fargo was struck speechless. He stared at the hole in her belly and imagined the slug bouncing around inside her and felt sick.

"Ain't that funny?" Alice said softly. "Me in the family way, and no family. No man I love with all my heart. Only a bastard who raped me and left me lying there like so much trash."

Fargo forced his vocal cords to work. "Who?"

"What difference does it make?" Alice returned. "Me and the baby are goners."

"This is why you've been out for blood," Fargo said. "It was more than being arrested and the chains and the work gang."

"They were part of it," Alice said, "but mostly this."

"Who?" Fargo asked again. He was over his shock.

Fargo frowned. A familiar hardness was coming over him, a hardness that had nothing to do with beds and gushing and such.

Alice seemed to turn her gaze inward even as her body seemed to shrivel in on itself. "He caught me by surprise. After more than two years with no one laying a hand on me, I didn't figure anyone would."

"I'd like to know."

Alice was silent awhile, more tears trickling. She took a deep breath and shuddered and said, "There I was, out to the Stoddard Ranch, like usual. The men were digging another damn ditch. Me, I'd been told to help out around the house. Make the beds and sweep the floors and wash the dishes. Just like a damn maid."

Fargo didn't interrupt. She had to tell it at her own pace.

"I hated it. Hated that bitch looking down her nose at me like I was no-account. And you wonder why I blew her head off. Because she did worse." Alice paused. "She was in on it. She told me to remake the bed in the guest room, they called it. I went in and the bed was fine. I couldn't understand why she wanted it redone." She paused again. "That was when he came up behind me and grabbed me."

The horror in her voice reached deep into Fargo and lit his veins with fire.

"He threw me on the bed. I fought. God, how I fought. But I'm a little thing and he was a grown man and he forced me down and had his way." Alice sobbed, just once. "And you know what? In the middle of it, when it was as bad as it could be, I heard her laugh out in the hall. That bitch. The one you said I shouldn't have shot. She laughed at what he was doing to me."

"You should have told me sooner."

"Why? It's personal. It's none of anyone's business but my own. I'm not one of those silly females that prattles about every little thing that happens to them."

"This wasn't little."

"No," Alice agreed, "it surely wasn't. Now that I think about it, he probably picked me because at the time Sarabeth was the only other woman in the chain gang and she's long at the tooth."

She was quiet awhile, until Fargo said, "Alice?"

"I'm only telling you now because I hate to die without anyone knowing."

"So that's why I'm still breathing."

"It was mine to do and I failed. You're free and clear and should keep on riding. Get on with your life."

"I'm not stupid," Fargo said.

She managed a grin. "Never figured you were, despite what I said about you being a stump."

"You could have let me go back into town. But you brought me all this way."

"To tell you."

"You want a hell of a lot more than that," Fargo said, not unkindly.

"I'm hopeful," Alice said, "but I don't know you all that well. It could be I'm wasting my breath."

"You're not."

Alice coughed, and nodded, and wept.

Fargo got up. He stepped to her side, sat back down, set the Henry next to his leg, and draped an arm around her shoulders. Without saying a word she rested her cheek on his shoulder and closed her eyes and continued to cry.

His throat constricted. He gazed out over the beauty of Texas without seeing it, and even though the temperature climbed as the sun rose, inside he was cold as ice.

It was a good while before Alice quieted and sniffled and wiped her nose with her sleeve. "Sorry," she said. "I reckon I'm weak."

"You're one of the strongest people I've ever met," Fargo said.

"It just ain't fair."

"No," Fargo said. "It's not."

"I think him and her were doing it."

"Gwendolyn Stoddard?"

"Who else? The way she set it up so he could. How she laughed about it. I think they were doing it behind her pa's back. I suspect she likes her pokes, that gal."

"For the last goddamn time, who?"

Alice sucked in a breath. "The tin star himself. Marshal Luther Mako."

"I'm surprised," Fargo admitted.

"Why? Because he acts so law and order? He puts on a great act. But as God is my witness, it was him who raped me."

"I believe you."

"You'll do what needs doing?"

Fargo mustered a grin of his own. "If you'll let me have my Henry."

Alice started to laugh and broke into a fit. Red flowed from her mouth and over her chin.

Fargo held her until the spasms stopped. He smoothed her hair and shifted and lowered her head to his lap.

She smiled weakly. "I'm glad I missed you out at the ranch."

"Anyone you want me to get word to?"

"No," Alice said. "Let my kin think I vanished off the face of the earth. I don't want them knowing I was raped."

"I wouldn't tell them that part."

Alice gently squeezed his arm. The effort set her to coughing and when she stopped she said, "You're a good man, Skye Fargo."

"Like hell."

"It wouldn't do if Mako is the only one," Alice said. "It will just go on and on, with more folks ending up like us. You savvy that, don't you?"

Fargo nodded.

A look of contentment came over her. "I can rest easy now." She folded her hands on her bosom. "Strange. The pain has mostly gone away."

"Good."

"My mouth sure is bone dry."

"I have a canteen."

"No need," Alice said. "It won't be long. I'd rather just lie here."

"Damn it all."

Alice reached up and touched his cheek. "Listen to you. Not that long ago you'd have shot me dead if you could."

"Don't remind me."

"Rest easy," she said. "So long as they're going to pay, I die happy." She closed her eyes and lowered her arms to her sides and was still.

"Alice?"

Her chest wasn't moving.

"Alice?" Fargo said again, and pressed her neck where there should be a pulse. There wasn't any. "Damn," he said.

The sun climbed and a bee buzzed around them, and Fargo didn't move.

He might have sat there the rest of the day, but the harsh cry of a circling hawk roused him into carefully placing her on the ground and rising.

He reckoned that right there was as good a place as any.

There was nothing to dig with, so he walked to the trees and found a downed limb long enough and thick enough for his purpose.

It was arduous work. The ground was hard.

Soon he was wet with sweat. Drops dripped into his eyes and stung like hell.

He dug a deep hole, out of respect, so the scavengers couldn't get at her.

As he worked, he pondered, and the more he pondered, the madder he became.

Long ago life had taught him that folks weren't always as they seemed. A stranger could be all smiles and as friendly as a parson, yet stab you in the back the moment you turned around.

People wore many faces, and the faces they showed to the world weren't necessarily who they were.

Then, too, some were outright hypocrites.

Horatio Stoddard, for instance. He claimed to have only the interests of his town at heart, but what he liked most was power and what he was really after was free labor for his ranch.

Then there was Marshal Luther Mako. He liked to say

he only cared about the law, but he had a dark side as vicious as any outlaw's. And he hid it so well, Fargo would never have suspected if not for Alice Thorn.

Finally there had been Alice herself. A small, freckled, frail-looking country girl, with more sand than most anyone. A proud woman who'd valued her dignity more than anything. Who wouldn't just ride off and forget she'd been violated. She'd aimed to make those who abused her pay in blood.

Fargo admired that. He admired it a whole hell of a lot.

He wasn't a cheek turner, either. Never had been, never would be. Cheek turning was for yellow-bellies and those who figured they were better than everyone else.

Presently the hole was long enough and deep enough. He carried Alice over and set her on the grass next to it, then got his bedroll from the Ovaro, spread out a blanket, placed Alice on it, and wrapped her from head to toe.

He cut his rope and tied the blanket at both ends. It would have to do in lieu of a casket.

Fargo folded his hands and tried to come up with words to say. He couldn't quote the Bible, like some. And he hardly knew a lick of poetry.

He settled for "She was a good woman. She didn't deserve this shit."

He placed her in the hole and covered it.

By the time he was done, he was covered with dust. He swatted it off with his hat, shoved the Henry into his saddle scabbard, and was ready to head out.

"I'll do what has to be done," Fargo said to the mound of dirt.

By then it was afternoon.

He had a long ride ahead.

Climbing on the Ovaro, Fargo snagged the reins to her horse and headed for Fairplay.

A reckoning was due.

24

The three riders drew rein and waited for him. The tin stars they wore were bright and shiny.

Fargo had never laid eyes on them before. New deputies, he figured, to replace those Alice Thorn had bucked out in gore. He rode right up to them and stopped and waited for them to set the tumbleweed rolling.

City bred, these threes. Their clothes, their hats, were store bought. They had pasty pink faces, and were overweight and looked about as harmless as babies.

But each had a revolver strapped around his waist, and as Fargo came up, each placed a hand on it.

The man in the middle wore a bowler and a tie and was sweltering in the heat but didn't have the sense to undo it. "This is a surprise."

"Is it?" Fargo said.

"My name is Clogburn. I've been appointed a deputy by Marshal Luther Mako."

"Is that a fact?"

"Someone saw you and the woman leave town and we've been following your tracks as best we can, and here you are."

"Here I am," Fargo said.

The other two were uneasy and it showed. One bit his bottom lip. The other's face kept twitching.

"We're to place you and that female under arrest."

"Her name was Alice Thorn."

"Was?" Clogburn said.

Fargo nodded at the empty saddle on the sorrel. "She's dead. Your marshal shot her. He raped her, too."

Disbelief twisted Clogburn's face. "Luther Mako did no such thing. I've known him for years. He's a straight arrow if ever there was one."

"Alice was pregnant with his baby," Fargo said. "He killed both of them with the same slug."

"You're lying, mister," said the man who had been biting his lip. "That doesn't sound like anything the marshal would do."

"It sure doesn't," declared the third deputy.

Fargo sighed. "I'm not in the mood."

"I beg your pardon?" Clogburn said.

"Jackasses," Fargo said. "I've had my fill of them." He let go of the sorrel's reins.

"We're not, neither," Clogburn said.

"I'm riding on to town. Get out of my way or you won't like what happens."

"You can't talk to us like that," Clogburn said, and tapped his badge. "We're deputies."

"And we don't like being insulted," said the third man.

"Give us your six-shooter and that rifle I see poking out of your scabbard and we'll take you in," Clogburn said. "I give you my word you won't come to harm."

"You don't want to push," Fargo said.

"Mister, you have your gall. We're the law. You're a fugitive who has escaped from custody. You don't get to tell us what to do. We get to tell you."

"Do you have families?"

Clogburn cocked his head. "What if we do?"

"You need to ask yourselves if they can get along without you."

"You dirty cur," the third man said. "Trying to scare us into not doing our jobs."

"You're not real lawmen," Fargo said.

"We were deputized," Clogburn said. "We took an oath and swore to uphold the law." He held out a hand. "Now let's have that smoke wagon, or else."

Fargo knew a lost cause when he heard one. These men weren't his enemies, but he'd be damned if he'd let them take him in and more damned if he'd turn his hardware over to them. "It will have to be the 'or else.'"

"You picked it," Clogburn said. He looked at the other two and nodded.

They drew, or at least they started to.

Not one had cleared his holster when the Colt was in Fargo's hand. He fanned a shot into Clogburn's shoulder and another into the deputy on the right and a third into the last.

The men on either side pitched from their mounts, but Clogburn stayed on, clutching himself and his saddle horn, blood spurting between his fingers. "You shot me!"

"I'll do it again if you don't shed that hog leg."

With panicked speed, Clogburn threw his six-shooter as far as he could.

The man who had bit his lip was still, but the last one was trying to unlimber his revolver even though Fargo's slug had smashed his gun arm.

"Let it be, you peckerwood."

"I'll kill you," the man hissed.

"If that's how you want it," Fargo said, and shot him in the chest.

"The mayor will see that you hang for this," Clogburn said.

Gigging the Ovaro up next to Clogburn's horse, Fargo slammed the Colt against the townsman's temple.

Clogburn thudded to the high grass.

Fargo rode on. They could tend to themselves or die, for all he cared. He left the sorrel there.

Thankfully he didn't encounter more deputies before Fairplay sprouted from the plain.

The sun was close to setting and a golden glow lent the town a false sheen of beauty.

Fargo sought cover in some cottonwoods and waited for dark. He didn't delude himself about his prospects. More than likely they'd shoot him on sight.

He thought of Alice with that bullet hole in her belly, and said to himself, "Let them try."

He made sure the Colt was reloaded and that the Henry had fifteen in the tube magazine.

Twilight fell, and lights sparked to life in dozens of windows.

Fargo didn't budge until it was so dark he could barely see his hand at arm's length. There was no moon, and clouds obscured a lot of the stars.

Circling to the west, he warily drew nearer.

The streets were quiet. It was the supper hour. Most folks were at home.

Hugging the shadows, Fargo made his way to the barracks. He stayed in the saddle and peered in the barred windows.

The prisoners were seated on their bunks talking or sprawled in exhaustion.

Climbing down, Fargo drew his Colt. He stepped to the jail and without hesitating opened the back door and strode in as if he belonged there.

Deputy Brock and another deputy were at the desk.

Brock was in the chair, his shirt off, his right shoulder bandaged. He wasn't wearing a gun belt.

They stopped talking, and Brock gaped in bewilderment. "It can't be."

"Miss me?" Fargo said.

"You must have brass balls."

"So did Alice Thorn."

"What?"

"Who is this?" the other man said. He was skinny with stooped shoulders and a hooked nose.

"Didn't you hear the marshal describe him?" Brock said. "This here is Fargo, the hombre we're after. Him and that female he mentioned."

The man had the brains of a gnat. "Fargo!" he cried, and did the last thing he should have. He clawed for his six-gun.

Fargo didn't want to shoot if he could help it. The blasts would bring the curious. He took two long bounds and struck the man on the head so hard that the man's hat went flying and his knees gave out.

Deputy Brock swore and went to stand.

"I wouldn't," Fargo said, leveling his Colt.

"You made a mistake waltzing in here. All it will take is for someone to look in the window and see you and they'll go for help."

Fargo was all too aware of that. He indicated the back door. "Grab the keys."

"Not *again*?"

"If at first you don't succeed," Fargo said.

"Mako will only round them up like he did before," Brock said. "You're wasting your time."

"It's my time to waste," Fargo said, and moved aside.

Brock rose and took the ring from the peg on the wall. "Where did that little bitch get to? The one the mayor claims is helping you?" Jiggling the ring, he came around the desk.

"She's where Mako can never touch her again," Fargo said. "She asked me to give her regards."

"Was it her or you who winged me?"

"Quit yapping and move."

Brock took a step past, then suddenly spun and lashed the keys at Fargo's gun hand.

Fargo tried to jerk away, but pain exploded across his knuckles and the revolver went sliding across the floor. He turned to go after it only to have Brock spring in front of him.

"Well, now. Looks like I have the upper hand."

"Did you hear me give up?"

"Don't need to," Brock said. "I'm fixing to beat you until you beg me to stop."

"That will be the day."

"Let's find out."

The keys flashed at Fargo's eyes. Ducking, he pivoted and drove a right to Brock's ribs. It was like hitting iron bars. He rammed a left, to no effect.

Brock laughed and swung a backhand that clipped Fargo on the jaw. The force was enough to rock him back a step.

The big deputy came after him, lashing the keys at his face.

Fargo retreated, all too aware that Luther Mako or someone else might walk in at any moment. He dodged. He twisted.

Brock's boot caught him on the leg. Agony exploded, and he almost buckled.

"Not so tough without a six-shooter, are you?" Brock said. His shoulder wound didn't seem to be bothering him any.

His shoulder wound. Fargo sidestepped a swing and slammed his fist against the bandage.

Brock winced and recoiled. "You son of a bitch. You'd better not start me bleeding again."

"Let's hope," Fargo said. He feinted with his left and drove his right into the bandage.

Bellowing like a mad bull, Brock spread his arms wide and rushed him.

Skipping back, Fargo collided with a wall. Before he could leap out of the way, Brock was on him.

Brock's arms wrapped around his, pinning them, and he was bodily lifted off the floor. "I've got you now, tough guy."

Fargo strained to break free but couldn't.

"Here everyone is so scared of you, and you ain't nothing," Brock said. "Time to end this."

25

"It sure is," Fargo said. Snapping his head back, he smashed his forehead into Brock's nose.

The big deputy howled. Blood spurted over his mouth and chin and he let go.

Fargo slugged him twice on the jaw as hard as he'd ever hit any man, but Brock didn't go down.

Shaking his head, the deputy roared and came at him again.

Big men often relied on their size to carry them through a fight. Fargo was big himself, but he also relied on something Brock didn't possess: skill.

Fargo dodged the sweep of an arm and rammed punches to Brock's kidney. Brock cried out, stumbled. By now he was in a rage driven by pure bloodlust. He lunged at Fargo's throat and clamped a hand as tight as a vise.

"Now you die!"

"After you," Fargo said, and kicked him where it hurt any man the most.

Brock sagged and turned the color of a beet.

Slipping a slow punch, Fargo retaliated, twice. A big hand swept at his face and he blocked and rammed a fist to Brock's. A big foot drove at his crotch and he avoided it and landed four blows of his own.

Cursing, Brock threw the keys at him, turned, and ran toward the desk.

Fargo palmed the Arkansas toothpick. He reached Brock

just as the deputy opened a drawer and grabbed a revolver. The six-shooter swept toward him as he sank the toothpick in as far as it would go below Brock's sternum.

For a moment they were still, Brock wearing a look of utter surprise. Then Fargo yanked the toothpick out and the deputy crashed onto the desk, his weight causing it to slide half a foot. His body slid off and hit the floor with a splat.

Breathing heavily, Fargo leaned on the desk. Now there were only the two to do.

He wiped the toothpick on Brock's pants and slid it into it sheath.

A light tap at the window made him jump. A face peered in, and Fargo raised a hand in greeting and called out, "Come on in."

Carmody Wells had a shawl over her head and shoulders. She entered as if she were walking on eggs, unable to take her eyes off Brock. "I saw the whole thing."

"You were supposed to stay with Jugs," Fargo reminded her.

"It's been so long, I was worried about you."

"Where does the marshal live?"

"At a boardinghouse, but he's not there."

"How do you know?"

"Jugs was asking around earlier. She heard tell that Mako went with Stoddard to his ranch. Apparently the mayor didn't want to spend the night out there alone." Carmody paused. "I hear his daughter is dead."

"A lot of people are." Fargo picked up the keys, wiped off a few drops of blood, and held them out. "Do me a favor and go let the prisoners out of those chains."

"Why me?"

"Why not?"

Fargo swatted her fanny as she went by. He collected his Colt, then took a lantern off the wall and lit it. With that in one hand and the lamp in the other, he went out the back and over to the barracks.

Two of the men were free and Carmody was working on the third.

Framed in the doorway, Fargo addressed them. "This makes twice I've freed you. Get to the stable, help yourselves to horses, and ride like hell."

"Steal a horse?" one said. "That son of a bitch Stoddard will add five years to our time."

"You won't have to worry about him."

"And the marshal?" another man asked.

"You won't have to worry about him, either."

They stared and an older prisoner said, "You don't have to do it on our account."

"I'm not," was all Fargo said.

It took five minutes, but the last of the men cast off his chain.

That left Sarabeth.

Carmody brought her down the aisle with an arm over her shoulder.

"She doesn't want to go. She's afraid of what they'll do to her."

"Take her with you. Stick with the men until you reach the next town, then scatter."

"But I want to stay with Jugs."

"You do and the townsfolk are liable to catch you and tear you to pieces. Or tie you to a hitch rail like they did that other one."

"Then this is the last time I'll see you?"

"Light a shuck," Fargo said to all of them, "and don't look back."

The men needed no urging, but Carmody hesitated and placed a hand on his arm. "I've taken a powerful shine to you."

"We don't have all night."

"Damn it all, anyhow." Carmody kissed him on the cheek and led Sarabeth away.

Fargo waited until he heard hooves drum in the distance.

Then he walked to the partition and dashed the lantern to the floor. Coming back down, he did the same near the front door, and went out.

Once on the Ovaro, Fargo headed north. When he reached the edge of town, he looked back.

Flames were shooting into the night sky and clouds of smoke drifted like fog. With any luck the fire would spread to the jail before an alarm was spread.

It could be that neighboring buildings would go up and then more if they didn't organize a water brigade.

"Serves them right," Fargo said aloud, and brought the stallion to a gallop.

As he rode he thought of Alice Thorn. He thought of her condition. He thought of those who had been clapped in leg irons. He thought of his own trial, and of being behind bars. He thought of all that so that when he reached the lane, he was a cauldron about to boil over.

The ranch house was a black block. A horse nickered, and he spied it, tied to a porch rail. Mako's, he reckoned, and drew rein.

Swinging down, Fargo shucked his Colt instead of taking the Henry. He was going close in; he wanted to see their faces.

The lane was gravel and although he placed each boot lightly, a couple of times the gravel crunched.

He angled across the grass for a better view of the front of the house and heard a rasp. Almost too late he realized it was a window being raised and he threw himself flat as multiple spurts of flame and thunder sent lead his way.

Six shots, fired so swiftly it could only be one person.

Fargo started to crawl and was surprised when his name was hollered.

"You came back," Luther Mako said. "I gave you credit for more brains."

Fargo knew he shouldn't answer. But he had to. "I gave you credit for being better than you are."

"I'm as good with a six-gun as most anyone breathing," Mako bragged.

"You whip them out fast enough," Fargo conceded, and added, "The same as you do with your cock."

There was a short silence.

"So she told you," Mako said. "It was just the once. I don't know what came over me."

"I do," Fargo said. "Or have you forgotten you were screwing Stoddard's daughter?"

"How did you—?" Mako began, and caught himself.

From somewhere upstairs came a bellow from His Honor. "What was that? What did he just say about Gwendolyn?"

"One more thing," Fargo called out to the lawman. "Alice Thorn is dead. You killed her. Her and her baby both."

"Baby?" Mako said. "I didn't know. I swear to God I didn't."

Fargo wasn't listening. He was on the move, to the far side of the house. He covered the final ten feet in a sprint. His back to the wall, he peered in a window.

Inside, twin pistols boomed.

Fargo jerked back as the glass shattered and shards fell like rain. He fired twice, then raced to the rear and over to the back door.

They would be waiting for him.

Hiking his leg, Fargo kicked. It was bolted, as he figured it would be. His kick did no more than jar it.

Leaping aside, he ran back the way he had come as revolvers cracked and slugs tore through the door. He sprinted to the shattered window and was through and in the parlor.

Out in the hallway the Starr revolvers blasted twice more.

In the vicinity of the stairs, Horatio Stoddard's voice drifted down from the second floor. "Did you get the son of a bitch?"

"Shut the hell up," Mako growled. "I'll have a look-see."

Fargo crept to the hall. He couldn't see Stoddard, but Mako was midway to the back door. Fargo pointed his Colt at the middle of Mako's mass. With his other hand he thumped the floor.

Luther Mako spun, and Lord, he was quick. His revolvers were thunderclaps.

Fargo fired, thumbed back the hammer, fired again.

Mako lurched and those lightning pistols cracked twice.

Emptying the Colt, Fargo felt a sting.

The sudden silence was broken by the sound of a heavy body falling.

Fargo commenced to reload.

"Mako?" Horatio whispered. "Is he dead?"

From the hall came a ragged intake of breath.

"Damn it, Luther, answer me."

Feet scraped the stairs.

Fargo finished and quietly cocked the hammer. By now his eyes had adjusted and he saw Horatio Stoddard almost to the bottom with the shotgun to his shoulder.

Horatio moved to the lawman and made a clucking sound. "How could you let him do this to you? You were supposed to be one of the best."

By then Fargo was behind him. He touched the Colt to the nape of Horatio's neck and Horatio bleated and turned his head.

"Bye," Fargo said, and squeezed the trigger.

Holstering the Colt, Fargo picked up the shotgun and leveled it at the pasty face glaring up at him.

"I hope you rot in hell," Luther Mako croaked.

"You first," Fargo said.

The boom of booth barrels shook the walls.

Now there was only one thing left to do.

Fargo lit a lamp and rummaged in the kitchen and found a half-full bottle of whiskey. Opening it, he took a long pull, then dashed the lamp to the floor.

When he climbed on the Ovaro, three windows were aglow.

Fargo nodded and tapped his spurs. It was a long ride to anywhere, and the night was young.

LOOKING FORWARD!
The following is the opening section of the next novel in the exciting Trailsman series from Signet:

TRAILSMAN #381
BOWIE'S KNIFE

1861, the Texas border country—to get there is hard enough, to make it out alive even harder.

They were one day out of San Gabriel when the bandidos struck.

Skye Fargo had called a halt on a low rocky rise. They were in desert country, and were grateful when the heat of the day gave way to the cool of night.

Fargo wasn't expecting trouble. As their guide, he had to keep an eye out for hostiles and outlaws, and he'd seen nothing to suggest they were in danger.

A big man, broad at the shoulders and narrow at the hips, Fargo wore garb typical of his profession: buckskins. He was a scout by trade, although that wasn't all he did. He also wore a dusty white hat, a red bandanna, and scuffed boots. Strapped around his waist was a Colt that had seen a lot of use, and propped against the saddle next to him was a Henry rifle.

A coffee cup in his left hand, Fargo was admiring one of the members of their party over the rim.

Lustrous chestnut hair framed a pear-shaped face. She had full, luscious lips, an aquiline nose, and eyes as vivid blue as Fargo's own. Her riding outfit, which included a pleated skirt, complemented her hourglass figure and full bosom. Dandelion Caventry was her name, and just looking at her was enough to set Fargo to twitching below his belt.

"How in hell did you get a handle like Dandelion, any-how?" he wondered.

"I much prefer Dandy," she said in her Texas twang. "My mother is to blame. Dandelions were her favorite flower as a little girl, so when she had one of her own . . ." Dandy grinned and shrugged.

"Thank God she wasn't fond of horse shit."

Dandy laughed heartily, but the man sitting next to her didn't. He was enough like her that it was obvious they were related. He wore a tailored suit and a derby and a perpetual scowl. "You shouldn't use that kind of language in the presence of a lady."

"Horses do shit," Fargo said.

Dandy tittered.

"That's not the point and you know it," the man said angrily. "You're much too crude for my tastes, Mr. Fargo. Much too crude by half."

"Enough, Lester," Dandy said. "I wasn't offended. And I don't need my brother to defend me."

"You shouldn't have to hear that word," Lester insisted.

"Shit?" Fargo said, and did some laughing of his own. "Boy, you have a lot to learn."

"Don't call me that," Lester said. "You're not much older than I am."

"I'm old enough to say shit."

Dandy cackled, but her brother only became madder. Balling his fists, Lester Caventry glanced at the two men who sat across the fire from them.

"Are you just going to sit there and let him abuse us? Am I the only one with a shred of decency?"

One of the men had a pale moon of a face and was heavy-set. The other was taller with a walrus mustache. Their clothes were store bought and far less expensive than Lester's. Each wore a bowler and each wore a revolver that his hand was always near.

"What would you have us do, Mr. Caventry?" asked the one with the moon face. Bushy brows poked from under his bowler like twin hairy caterpillars trying to crawl up his face.

"You can insist that our guide show proper manners to my sister," Lester said. "What does my father pay you for, anyhow, Mr. Bronack? You, too, Mr. Waxler?"

"Your father," Bronack said, "is paying us to protect the two of you from any and all threats, and see to it that the knife, if it's genuine, reaches him safely."

"He never said we were to protect you from dirty words," Waxler said.

Fargo snorted.

"You don't amuse me, Mr. Waxler," Lester said. "And what could happen to the knife, anyhow?"

"Honestly, brother," Dandy said. "If it is, in fact, *the* knife, it's worth a small fortune."

"Which is what Father is willing to pay for the stupid thing," Lester said bitterly.

"Don't start with that again," Dandy said.

Fargo sighed. Ever since leaving Austin, he'd had to put up with their spats. Some brothers and sisters didn't get along, and these two were always carping. To be fair, Lester did a lot more of it than Dandy. So much, in fact, several times along the way he'd been tempted to bean the sourpuss with a rock.

"I still think you should stand up for my sister's virtue." Lester directed his spite at Bronack and Waxler. "Is it too much to ask that those in our company act like gentlemen?" He gave Fargo a pointed glare.

"Honestly, brother," Dandy said.

Fargo was about to tell Lester that he could take his holier-than-thou attitude and shove it up his ass when the Ovaro raised its head and nickered.

Fargo was instantly alert. His stallion wasn't prone to skittishness. Something—or someone—was out there. Something—or someone—had agitated it. He probed the desert below the rise but saw only the ink of night.

Without being obvious about it, Fargo shifted his right arm so his hand brushed his Colt. "Bronack, Waxler," he said quietly.

The pair caught on right away. They didn't jump up in alarm. They were professionals. Each eased his hand to his six-shooter and slowly gazed about.

"What is it?" Lester asked much too loudly.

"Shut the hell up," Fargo said. "Don't move unless I say to. You and your sister, both."

"Now, see here—" Lester began.

"Do as he says," Dandy intervened. "Father hired him because he's the best there is at what he does."

Fargo caught movement to the west and then to the east. Whoever was out there had the rise hemmed and was closing in. "When I tell you," he said to the Caventrys, "drop on your bellies and stay down until the shooting stops."

"What shooting?" Lester asked in confusion.

A shape rushed out of the night, the glint of a rifle in its hands. A muzzle was thrust toward them and the man shouted in Spanish, *"Nadie se mueva! Les hemos rodeado!"*

Like hell, Fargo thought. He drew as he dived and thumbed off a shot. The slug caught the man high in the chest and sent him crashing to the hard earth.

Half a dozen other shapes materialized. Rifles and pistols cracked and boomed.

Bronack and Waxler sprang to Dandy and Lester to protect them while blasting away.

Fargo saw a figure charge up and fanned two swift shots. He went for the head. Hair and brains spewed out the crown of a sombrero, and the figure tumbled.

As quickly as the attack commenced, it fizzled. The rest whirled and bolted, firing a few wild shots. Their footsteps rapidly faded.

Fargo rose into a crouch. "Anyone hit?"

"I'm fine," Dandy said.

"I'm not," Lester said. "I heard one of the bullets go right past my ear."

"Did it crease you?" Dandy asked.

"No, but it scared the daylights out of me."

It was a shame, Fargo reflected, that some people gave birth to jackasses.

Bronack and Waxler straightened. Bronack was unhurt, but Waxler had been nicked in the left arm. "It's nothing," he said. "I'll bandage it and be good as new."

Fargo went to the man he'd shot in the head. The grubby clothes, the stubble, the bandoleer with half the loops empty marked him as surely as if he wore a sign. "Bandidos."

"Here and now?" Lester said. "Wouldn't they have been smarter to attack us in the daytime?"

"They'd have been smart to pick us off from out in the dark," Fargo said. That they hadn't was peculiar. Or maybe the bandits wanted them alive to whittle on. Except for Dandy. They'd undoubtedly put her to a different use.

"We were lucky," Bronack said.

"I can't quite believe it happened," Dandy said. "It was over so fast."

"It happened, all right." Fargo kicked the body. "Here's your proof." He went through the man's pockets, but all he found was a folding knife with two blades, one of which was broken. Moving to the other one, he did the same and wound up with a handful of pesos.

"Shouldn't we douse the fire in case they come back?" Lester asked anxiously.

"They won't," Fargo said.

"How can you be so sure?"

"Three guesses." Fargo glanced at Bronack. "Keep them here and keep them quiet."

With that, staying low, Fargo glided down the rise and crouched at the bottom. He could make out some creosote and yucca, and to his left, mesquite. The bandits had fled to the south. He crept after them, careful to stop and listen often. He'd gone maybe a hundred yards when he heard what he'd hoped to hear: the drum of hooves, dwindling. He crept on and came to a wash. An acrid scent tingled his nose. At the bottom lay the stub of a smoldering cigar.

Fargo descended. This was where the bandits had left their mounts. Trying to follow them would be pointless. He couldn't track at night without a torch, and they'd see him coming from miles off.

"Damn," Fargo said. He would have liked to show them how he felt about folks trying to kill him.

He took his time returning to the rise. It was nice to be by himself. He was tired of listening to Lester complain about everything under the sun.

Lester was a baby in a man's body. Fargo reckoned this

came from being born with silver spoon in his mouth. Their pa, Stephen Augustus Caventry, was one of the wealthiest hombres in Texas. Hell, he was one of the richest anywhere. A shipping line, a stage line, and other interests had filled his coffers to bursting.

Lester and Dandelion never wanted for anything their whole young lives. That fact hadn't affected Dandy much, but her brother thought the whole world had been created just for him.

Fargo had seldom met anyone who had his head so far up his own ass.

Another two weeks or so and he would be shed of them. That was how long it should take to reach San Gabriel, get what they came for, and light a shuck for Austin.

It had surprised him, Lester saying they were after a knife. No one had told him. Not Stephen Caventry, who'd offered him a thousand dollars to conduct his grown daughter and son to the border country and back. Not Dandy, who was friendly enough but not as friendly as he'd like. And not Lester, who gave the impression he thought they were on a fool's errand.

Fargo was so deep in thought, he'd let down his guard. The crunch of a foot behind him almost came too late. He started to turn even as a hand fell on his shoulder.

GRITTY WESTERN ACTION FROM

USA TODAY **BESTSELLING AUTHOR**
RALPH COTTON

Available wherever books are sold or at
penguin.com

S909

National bestselling author

RALPH COMPTON

"A writer in the tradition of Louis L'Amour and Zane Grey!" —*Huntsville Times*

Available wherever books are sold or at
penguin.com

S543

NEW IN HARDCOVER

THE LAST OUTLAWS
The Lives and Legends of Butch Cassidy and the Sundance Kid

by Thom Hatch

Butch Cassidy and the Sundance Kid are two of the
most celebrated figures of American lore. As leaders of
the Wild Bunch, also known as the Hole-in-the-Wall
Gang, they planned and executed the most daring
bank and train robberies of the day, with an
uprecedented professionalism.

The Last Outlaws brilliantly brings to life these
thrilling, larger-than-life personalities like never before,
placing the legend of Butch and Sundance in the
context of a changing—and shrinking—American
West, as the rise of 20th century technology brought
an end to a remarkable era. Drawing on a wealth of
fresh research, Thom Hatch pushes aside the myth and
offers up a compelling, fresh look at these icons of the
Wild West.

**Available wherever books are sold or at
penguin.com**

S0464